CAREY'S VENGEANCE

Thomas Carey Westerns
Book Two

Irving A Greenfield

CAREY'S
VENGEANCE

Published by Sapere Books.

24 Trafalgar Road, Ilkley, LS29 8HH

saperebooks.com

ISBN: 978-1-80055-769-7

ONE

Lieutenant Thomas Carey was captured on the south side of the Chickahominy River by a Union patrol, who happened upon him just as he and another man were fighting.

'Near as I make out,' the sergeant said, stroking his full black beard and at the same time shifting his eyes from the prisoner to Captain Sheely, his company commander, 'they wuz out ta kill each other from the start.' He turned his eyes back to the reb. 'I spots the three of 'im long be-fer the lootenant and that Zeb fella started fightin' —'

'Who the hell is Zeb?' Captain Sheely asked. So far, he couldn't make heads or tails out of the sergeant's report.

As for the prisoner's version of what happened, the captain doubted that it would be any less confused. In fact, he was quite sure that even though the man was an officer, his ability to communicate would prove to be practically nil. It seemed to him that the prisoner was scarcely aware of his surroundings, to say nothing about his particular situation. After all, the circumstances of his capture were most peculiar …

If it wasn't for that bizarre aspect, the captain would have remanded the prisoner to the stockade and that would have been the end of it. Any interrogation would have been done by the commander of the stockade the following morning. But to protect himself, lest he be called by his superiors for having been derelict in his duty — as well as to satisfy his curiosity — he decided to not only take his sergeant's report but also to question the prisoner himself.

'The man the lootenant kilt … like I wuz tellin' you,' the sergeant continued, looking at the captain again after a long pause, 'I sees the two rebs comin' toward the narrow part of the river. Then this third rider comes up behind 'im. He moved in real close and he throwed his knife at the man behind the lootenant. Then he and the lootenant started at each other. I've been soldierin' for as long as there's been a war, an' I tell you I never seen anythin' like what I saw the lootenant do to him.' He looked at the prisoner again and shook his head. 'No sir, I never seen anythin' like that! The lootenant kilt him with this,' he said, pulling a roweled spur out of his pocket and giving it to the captain.

'For the love of God, man,' the captain exclaimed, 'will you tell me what happened!' He examined the spur and then looked at the prisoner, who still appeared to be oblivious to everything.

'Well, sir,' the sergeant said, 'it wuz too dark an' misty fer me ta see everythin', and I wuz too far away from 'im fer me ta hear what they wuz sayin', but the next thin' I knowed they were clawin' at each other. As soon as that happened, I got real close … they wuz too busy fightin' to pay much heed to anythin' else. I heard the lootenant ask Zeb who sent him. Seems like they knew each other for a long time … Zeb won't say … The lootenant becomes real angry and he uses that there spur on Zeb's throat. I guess that makes Zeb change his mind … that's when he tells him it was the lootenant's pa.'

'His father?' Sheely asked with disbelief.

'Yep, his pa,' the sergeant said, shaking his head. 'Don't seem real, but I wuzn't the only one who heard it.'

The captain felt a sudden rush of goose bumps down his back. He had heard that family ties in the South were incredibly strong, but what the sergeant had just told was apparently the exception. He looked at the roweled spur, and then at the prisoner. The man was tall, lean and raw-boned, and even in the yellow glow from the coal oil lamp on the desk, his eyes were decidedly green.

Sheely realized that though the prisoner was probably in his early twenties§§ there was something very, very old about him — or was it a characteristic other than age in the man's face? Sheely looked down at the spur. For a man to be able to kill with that, he would have to be hard, very hard indeed. He raised his eyes and studied the prisoner for some time, trying to decide what kind of man he was.

Thomas Carey stood very still, but not at attention. Though he could hear what the sergeant was saying, he didn't pay much attention to it. He was more interested in the sound of the rain as it beat against the heavy canvas of the tent.

It had started to rain shortly after he was taken across the river and now, hours later, it was still raining. The rain was more of an enemy than the whole damn Yankee Army. The army was made up of men who could be fought and killed. But the rain, the goddamn rain was nothing but a cold wetness, mud and — he turned his eyes up to the apex of the tent and silently cursed the rain.

'Lieutenant?' the captain called, realizing he had to get on with the questioning.

Thomas lowered his eyes and looked at him. The yellow light from the coal oil lamp illuminated the captain. He was young and his hands were long. Probably inexperienced. But if he managed to stay alive for a while, he would learn how to lead men, how to kill.

'According to my sergeant's account,' Sheely said feeling uncomfortable under the prisoner's penetrating stare, 'you tore a man's throat open with your spur?'

Thomas kept silent.

The captain, who had been standing behind a small dun-colored field desk ever since the sergeant had brought the reb officer into the tent, was annoyed by the prisoner's intransigence and obvious lack of respect for a superior officer. He had heard that Southern officers were insubordinate and at times even insolent to their superiors.

Suddenly he realized that the lieutenant wasn't even standing at attention. This flagrant breach of military courtesy in the presence of an enlisted man was intolerable, and — if for no other reason than to ensure the proper attitude of respect from his sergeant — Sheely felt compelled to do something about it. He stepped around to the front of the desk and ordered the prisoner to stand at attention.

Thomas remained motionless, but he shifted his eyes to the sergeant for a few moments and then looked straight at the captain.

'I gave you an order, lieutenant,' the captain said sharply.

'Beggin' your pardon sir,' the sergeant interjected.

The captain glanced at him. 'Yes, what is it?' he asked.

'I don't think you're goin' to get 'im to stand at attention, sir.'

'And why the hell not?'

The sergeant shook his head. 'Rebs are jest that way, captain. They take a notion not ta do somethin' an' that's all there is ta it. They're kinda mulish in their ways.'

'Stubborn bastards, you mean,' Sheely commented looking at the prisoner again.

'Yes, sir,' the sergeant answered. 'I remember back in '62 at Antietam my outfit came face ta face with some rebs who run out of ammunition and by Gawd, they throwed bricks at us. Some troopers claim that rebs druther fight than fuck.' He started to laugh. 'But any man that feels that way has his wits addled.'

'Spare me your comments,' Sheely told him, embarrassed by the man's crudity. 'And as for you, lieutenant, let me remind you that you are a prisoner, and as such you are no longer a free man. I asked you a question which as yet you have not answered. Perhaps I didn't make myself clear. Therefore, I will repeat it, 'According to my sergeant's report, you killed a man by ripping open his throat with your roweled spur, is that so?'

Thomas said nothing.

'Lieutenant,' Sheely warned, 'the amenities of war will not prevent me from obtaining an answer to whatever question I ask.'

Thomas once more flicked his eyes toward the sergeant, but remained silent.

'Was Zeb the name of the man you killed?'

Thomas clenched his fists.

Sheely caught the movement. Satisfied that he had evinced a reaction, he nodded and said, 'Now tell me this, why did your father send a man to kill you, or rather —'

The captain never finished what he had started to ask. The moment he uttered the word 'father', Thomas made a low growling noise deep in his throat and sprang at Sheely. Gripping the captain's throat in his hands, Thomas tried to throttle him to death.

Sheely struggled to free himself and managed to cry out for help before being brought down to the floor of the tent.

'I'll kill you,' Thomas said in a low passionless voice. 'I'll kill you!' But even as he pressed his thumbs against the captain's windpipe, the sergeant came up behind him and, raising his revolver, brought it down on the back of Thomas' head.

His brain exploded into blackness. He fell to one side but did not know it.

Captain Sheely scrambled to his feet and rubbing his neck croaked, 'He tried to kill me … by God, I could have him shot for that … Sergeant, you were a witness … the man's mad!'

The sergeant looked down at the reb officer. 'Seems to me,' he said, facing the captain, 'that I told you all rebs are mulish. This one wuzn't no different.'

'But he tried to kill me!'

'Never had a chance,' the sergeant said, holstering his revolver. 'He wuz jest tetchy about some things.!'ll take him over to the prison compound … and, sir, I wouldn't tell anybody that a reb prisoner tried ta kill you. It'll make you look a might poorly in the eyes of the men.'

TWO

Thomas' world was filled with bright colors. The clear blue of the sky and the hot yellow of the afternoon sun … the salmon hue of the sunsets … even the darkness of the night with a bright white moon that turned the dry land and everything on it to silver. It was so vivid, so unbelievably real that he could almost step into it and be home again.

Back to Paso Diablo where Lisa would welcome him. Lisa … Lisa … how he longed for her … how much he wanted to feel the softness of her body against his…

His father was suddenly standing there in the doorway between the prison and his home.

'She's a whore!' the old man said. 'Helen is your wife.'

'I never loved her,' Thomas said. 'I never wanted to marry her.'

'She gave you a son.'

'I never loved her.'

'Helen is a good woman,' the old man said.

Thomas shook his head. On their wedding night when he brought Helen home, Zeb had come with two men…

'What do you want?' Thomas asked.

'Who is he?' Helen cried, cowering near her new husband.

'I'll tell you who I am,' Zeb said. 'I'm kin of the man 'e gunned down at da Broken 'Orn.'

'It was a fair fight,' Thomas said. 'You were there. You saw.'

Zeb had come for vengeance. He cut and branded Helen, and then his two friends took her into the bedroom and raped her. They left her disfigured for life.

Thomas had never wanted to marry Helen, but his father…

His father had sent Zeb all the way from Texas to kill him. His father wanted him dead.

The night mists on the Chickahominy were thick. Thomas fought with Zeb. They struggled until he finally brought Zeb down.

'Who sent you?' Thomas demanded to know.

At first Zeb wouldn't answer, but then he told him who it was.

In a rage, Thomas lifted his foot and brought his roweled spur down on Zeb's neck.

The man screamed and his body jerked up, blood gushing out of the wound.

'You lie!' Thomas shouted. 'You lie! He wouldn't do that to his own son.'

'God's own truth,' Zeb swore.

The hot anger passed. Thomas felt only hate for Zeb, for his father. He lifted his foot again and tore open more of Zeb's throat. 'Now tell me —'

'Your pa!' he laughed. 'Your pa!'

The words echoed and re-echoed over and over again in Thomas' skull. They came out of the blackness like great claws and tore at his brain. But soon the darkness began to sluice away.

The top of Thomas' head ached. Slowly he opened his eyes. Everything was fuzzy. But after a few moments, he was able to sense, more than actually see, that he was in a long narrow room. Some distance from him there was a coal oil lamp. A row of wooden pallets came into view. Almost at the same time, he became aware of the fetid odor. Unmistakably it resulted from the combination of unwashed bodies, human waste and decaying straw. He looked toward the yellowish light of the coal lamp again, and this time the dark figures of several men came into view. Thomas tried to move, but the stab of pain in the back of his head forced him to stop and utter a low groan.

'The lootenant 'as come to,' someone said.

Thomas could not see the man. But nonetheless, he asked, 'Where am I?'

His question evoked a short burst of laughter from several of the men who were standing close to the coal oil lamp. Then one of the men stepped away from the others and said, 'One thin' is fer sure, lootenant, you ain't in 'eaven.'

More laughter!

'No, sir,' said the man, stopping in front of him, 'less'n' ya think a damn Yankee prison is 'eaven.'

With great effort, Thomas managed to pull himself up into a sitting position. Then sucking in his breath, he blinked several times and looked up. The man standing in front of him was tall and broad-shouldered. His big head was crowned by black hair, his beard was full and his lips were parted in a smile.

Thomas exhaled and nodded, lowering his eyes. He remembered now what had happened in the captain's tent.

'Ain't ya goin' to ask how long ya been 'ere?' the man said.

Thomas shook his head.

The man laughed and said, 'I guess it don't really make no difference, 'cause ya don't 'ave nowhere to go, 'cept to a prison camp up north somewhere.'

Several of the other men joined the big man in front of Thomas. All of them were ill-clothed, and a few had dirty bandages around their heads, arms and legs. They looked more like ghosts than men.

'How'd ya get your head busted open like that?' the big man asked.

'Looks like someone laid it open wid a —' one of the other men started to say.

'Let him tell us,' the big man said.

Thomas screwed his eyes up. Suddenly he realized his coat was gone and that the man in front of him was wearing it. He started to stand, but just as he got upright, the big man pushed him down.

'There weren't no need to do that, Jason,' one of the other men said.

'He's too weak to stand,' the big man answered with a laugh.

Thomas braced himself against the wooden pallet. It would be useless to say anything about his coat until he was strong enough to —

'Would you look at the way he's lookin' at me,' Jason laughed. 'I truly don't think the lootenant likes the idea of me takin' his coat.' He stopped laughing, reached down and, grabbing hold of the front of Thomas' tunic, pulled him halfway up to his feet. 'Listen,' he said, 'if'n I coulda pulled your boots off widout breakin' your leg, I'd a taken them too.' Then he flung Thomas down. 'We all are enlisted men here. You ain't no lootenant here.'

There was an immediate chorus of agreement from the other men.

'What d'you say to that?' Jason asked.

Thomas didn't even bother to look up. All his life he had come up against men like Jason. A Yankee prison was no different from any other place as far as that breed of man was concerned.

'You ain't answered me,' Jason said.

'Let him be!' someone suggested.

'Who said that?' Jason questioned, turning around.

'Me,' came the throaty answer.

The voice came from where there wasn't even a hint of light.

'Sounds like Mister Coomy,' Jason said, cocking his head to one side.

'That's right,' the man replied. 'Now I say let the lieutenant be!' This was immediately followed by a violent fit of coughing.

After a few moments, the knot of men standing in front of Jason made way for a slightly built man with a cadaverous face and glowing eyes. He was dressed in civilian clothes and walked very slowly. When he reached Jason, he stopped.

'He's got to know the rules,' Jason told him. 'I don't want him to get any wrong ideas 'cause he's a lootenant.'

'All right, you told him … Now let him alone.' Coomy sidestepped Jason and moved directly in front of Thomas.

'Get him to say so,' Jason demanded, turning toward Thomas again.

'For the love of God, lieutenant,' Coomy whispered, 'answer the man or he will keep at you.'

Thomas nodded.

'He nodded,' Coomy announced. 'He understands … Jason, now you know he understands.'

'Yeah,' Jason answered. 'I seen him nod. But I also seen the way he looked at me.'

'The man nodded,' Coomy insisted. 'He knows who and what you are.'

'He better not forget it,' Jason said, turning around and slowly walking away.

Coomy waited until Jason was out of earshot and even then he whispered. 'Under the circumstances you did the wisest thing possible.'

'Who are you?' Thomas questioned.

'A prisoner,' Coomy replied with a thin smile, 'like yourself.'

If for no other reason than he wore civilian clothes, Thomas doubted him. But he was beholden to Coomy and did not think of pressing for more of an explanation than the man had already given. With a nod, he accepted Coomy's answer. Then he lay back and closing his eyes, quickly drifted off into a deep sleep.

By the day after his capture, Thomas was already fit enough to start thinking about how he was going to escape. He discovered that the prison compound was rectangular, and that it was located on the top of a hill several miles from the imaginary line that divided the two contending armies.

The shelter for the prisoners consisted of a long narrow log building, with one door and several rough cut-outs that served as windows. The door faced the only gate that allowed the blue-bellies to enter and leave the compound, which they did at noon to bring two huge pots of watery soup and a small sack of hard tack.

At each of the four vertices of the rectangle stood a watch tower, whose access was on the other side of the ten-foot-high palisade that enclosed the prison area. From the other men, Thomas learned that there were always guards in the towers and at least two guards outside the gate. Other than the daily bringing of food, the prisoners were left to their own devices. Every one of them knew that they were just occupying a piece of Yankee space for a time before they would be sent to one of the big prison camps further north.

It was immediately obvious to Thomas that Jason was in command of a group of men much like himself, but who, lacking his physical size and strength, were eager enough to do Jason's bidding in return for his protection. When food was brought to the compound, it was Jason and his followers who took what they wanted first, and then the other men scrambled for the dregs that were left. Invariably it was Jason who got whatever scraps of meat the prison cook saw fit to throw into the cauldron.

The first time Thomas left his pallet to queue up for food, he went straight for the place in the yard where the blue-bellies set the pot down. He saw that Jason and some of the other men were already there, but was unaware that the other prisoners were purposely hanging back.

Coming up to the pot, Thomas dipped his tin cup into the hot watery broth and managed to snag a sickly grayish-colored piece of meat that was floating near the cup. Just as he was about to remove the cup from the pot, someone stayed his hand and said, 'Not your time yet, lootenant.'

With his free hand, Thomas shoved the man in the chest.

'Now jest a minute there, lootenant,' Jason said, stepping closer to him. 'He's only doin' what I told 'im to do.'

'Tell him to let go of my hand,' Thomas answered.

Jason shook his head. 'Can't do that,' he said.

Thomas looked away from Jason.

'It's not your time to eat yet. Ya gotta wait till me an' my friends eat.'

It was then that Thomas sensed a sudden tension in the yard. He saw that the other men in the compound were nowhere near the spot, but were waiting for Jason and his followers to finish before they came forward. Thomas' first impulse was to object and stand his ground. Almost within the same few moments, he realized that while he was talking, several of Jason's men had moved behind him. Though he had recovered sufficiently from the blow on his head to hold his own in a physical contest with Jason — perhaps even best him — he could not hope to fight the half-dozen men at the pot and still hope to get away with nothing more serious than a bad beating. The odds were too great. Intuitively he knew they would try to kill him. He decided that it was not the time or the place to make his move.

'Well, lootenant,' Jason questioned, 'you goin' ta be polite as befittin' your rank or —'

Thomas tilted the cup and poured the soup back into the pot.

Jason roared with laughter. 'You sure larn fast, lootenant … you sure larn fast.' He nodded, and the men who had circled behind Thomas moved back to the other side of the pot.

Thomas smiled and said, 'I hope when your time comes, Jason, you will learn as fast.' And before Jason could answer, he turned and moved away.

'What d'ya mean, lootenant?' Jason called after him.

But without looking back, Thomas continued to walk.

The only exception to Jason's rule that he and his men have first choice at the pot was Mr Coomy. He had free and immediate access to the food whenever he wished, as Thomas discovered in the ensuing days. But he ate very little. Mostly he stayed in the darkest part of the barracks.

After his initial intercession on Thomas' behalf, Coomy made no other attempt to be friendly or even speak with him. But his hacking cough frequently broke the silence of the night. It took Thomas the better part of a week to discover why Jason afforded Coomy special treatment.

The information came piecemeal from the other men, and even when Thomas put it all together, he knew only a few things about the man. Firstly, that Coomy had been a Confederate spy, or so the Yankees thought; secondly that he had been a gambler; third — and this he came to on his own — the man was dying of the lung disease. But since Coomy kept his relationship with Thomas to no greater display than an acknowledging nod, Thomas made no effort to get any closer.

In fact, he sought neither companionship nor conversation from the other men in the compound.

A greater part of his days was spent thinking about how to escape, and much of the night was given over to imagining how, when he returned to the ranch, he would tell his father about Zeb and then he would kill him. Sometimes, as he lay on his pallet and listened to the wheezing sounds, the coughing and the cries of those men who were reliving some moment of terror, Thomas would find himself wondering if Helen knew that his father had sent Zeb to kill him. There were nights when he was sure that she knew, but more often than not, Thomas believed she was innocent, though he realized that surely he had given her more than enough cause to want him dead.

By the end of the first week in the prison compound Thomas no longer felt the dull ache in the back of his skull. The weakness that had afflicted him in the days immediately after his arrival at the compound left him. But because of the lack of physical activity, his corded muscles seemed stiff and his joints hurt.

One day, late in the afternoon after a cloudy morning, the sun came out and he was leaning against the wall of the barracks hoping to feel some of its warmth. The weather had been wet and cold since his capture, and since the commander of the compound denied the prisoners the right to have a fire, they basked in the sun whenever it showed itself. It was the only way they had to warm themselves.

Thomas stood with his eyes closed. He could see his father very clearly. William Carey was a heavily built man with gray hair and a sharp-featured face the color of old leather.

'Now listen to me, Thomas,' William had said in a low but authoritative voice, 'you're going to stop seeing that woman in Paso Diablo —'

Thomas started to say something.

'You listen, I said,' William told him. 'I told Sam that you're going to marry Helen.'

'What?'

'You heard me,' William answered tightly. 'You're going to marry Helen and settle down before some man with a faster gun lays you out.'

'I can take care of myself,' Thomas growled. 'And I don't need you to find me a woman. I've already got a woman.'

'You've got a whore!' his father shouted. 'A damn half-breed bitch that will lay with any man if he has the price.'

Thomas started for his father with his hand raised to strike.

'Why not go for your gun?' William challenged, not moving an inch.

His words stopped Thomas, and he slowly lowered his hand. 'I am not going to do it,' he said. 'I have no feelings for Helen.'

'I'm not interested in your feelings,' William said. 'This ranch and half the Wickers' place will be yours. That should give you some feelings.'

Thomas shook his head. 'You don't have any right —'

'You're not of legal age yet,' William answered, 'so I guess I still have some rights.'

'But not to get me married to a woman —'

'Rather that than see you tied to that slut in Paso Diablo.'

'I love her.'

William snorted. 'You call wallowing in lust love?' he shouted. 'Why, she's just a bitch in heat and you're nothing more than a hound dog going after her.'

'I am not going to marry —'

'Either you marry Helen Wicker or you can clear out of here!' William growled. 'I'm doing what I think is best for you. Not only are you getting a good woman, but you're coming into a mighty nice piece of property, which is a helluva lot more than you deserve.'

'If you're so damn anxious to get hold of Sam's place,' Thomas yelled, 'why the hell don't you marry the bitch?'

Before William realized it, he moved and the back of his hand slammed against his son's face with such force that blood instantly streamed from the boy's nose. 'You'll marry her or you'll get out!' he said, breathing heavily.

Thomas' right hand had dropped to his gun. Had it been any other man who had struck him, he would have killed him. But he couldn't make his fingers curl around the gun. His hand trembled and fell to his side.

'Remember,' William said, realizing how far he had pushed Thomas, 'either you marry or you get out. Understand?'

Thomas drew his sleeve across the bottom of his nose and streaked it with blood.

'Do you understand?' William demanded to know.

That was the way his father was. Everything was black and white to him…

But Thomas couldn't give up the land. He couldn't give up what he had helped build, and he was sure that his father knew it. If there was anything between them, any bond that was stronger than blood, it was their mutual love for the land. But the way things had worked out, Thomas recognized that his love for the land had not only been used against him, but also had proved to be his weakness. Because of it he had married a woman he had not loved. But what was the sense of chewing over that?

He shrugged and, opening his eyes a bit, looked at the palisade. That wooden wall, and more than two thousand miles, stood between him and his father. But he would somehow get past that wall and travel the distance home, and he would do it to kill the old man. That much he owed him, and Thomas swore that he would do it.

He closed his eyes again and let his thoughts rabbit-hop from the possibility of scaling the palisade to how miserable he must look.

He rubbed his hand over his chin. There was more than just bristle there now. A beard was in the growing, a nesting place for more lice. Then he thought about Lisa. Conjuring the vision of her naked body made him lick his chapped lips. A surge of physical want passed through him and, sighing deeply, he knew that if he let the blue-bellies ship him north to a bigger prison camp, it would be years before he'd see Lisa — or, for that matter, any other woman.

'You must be thinking of something very sad,' Coomy said.

Thomas recognized who it was even before he opened his eyes and looked at him.

'Mind if I stand with you?' Coomy asked.

'Suit yourself,' Thomas said, and to show that he meant it, he moved along the rough log wall to make room for the man.

'You look as though you're all mended,' Coomy commented, turning his thin, sallow face toward the sun.

'Just as good as I was before,' Thomas assured him. He was puzzled by this unexpected intrusion into his solitude. He almost felt as though somehow Coomy had been able to see how much he longed for Lisa. But in the light of what the man had done for him that first night, he owed him some show of courtesy.

Mr Coomy was quiet for several minutes, and then, without moving his head or opening his eyes, he said, 'Word has gotten around that you killed a man. Some claim it was one of your own men.'

Thomas took a deep breath and sent it whistling out from between his lips. Now he knew why Coomy had come to pay him a visit.

'How did such word get around?' Thomas questioned.

Coomy lowered his head and, opening his eyes, looked at Thomas. 'The Yankees can keep us from getting out, but they can't keep some things from getting in. For a price a man can get tobacco, corn whiskey and even a woman, though for the last he is always taken out of the compound for special questioning.' He started to laugh, but quickly ended up coughing.

Thomas remained silent while Coomy was coughing. Then when the seizure passed, Coomy stepped away from the wall and, gathering a large glob of phlegm in his mouth, spit the bloody liquid out. When he returned to his former place against the wall, he apologized for not being more discreet about his condition.

Thomas nodded understandingly and then asked, 'How much do you know about what happened?'

'Nothing more than what I have already told you,' Coomy said with a shrug, 'except that you killed the man with your spur.'

'He was not a Confederate soldier,' Thomas said.

'Who was he?'

Thomas shook his head. 'A man from back home,' he replied.

'Some say he was a scout.'

'Hardly that,' he responded with a brittle laugh.

Coomy shrugged again and said, 'I thought you should know how things stand.'

'Meaning?'

'I came between you and Jason once,' Coomy said. 'But that time I knew I was right, and so did Jason and the rest of the men … now, if anything should start —'

'I can take care of myself,' Thomas told him swiftly. He was angered that Coomy would think he couldn't.

'Now that Jason knows —'

'He knows nothing,' Thomas responded sharply. 'Besides, it's none of his concern.'

Coomy shook his head and in a soft voice said, 'It has to be his concern … he'll make it his concern, especially since most of the men believe the man you killed was one of their own.'

'Let them think what they want to!'

'I'm afraid they will,' Coomy answered. 'But if it should come to anything between you and Jason, remember that he has the men on his side. And he also has a weapon.'

Thomas' eyes opened wide.

'A sharply pointed stick,' Mr Coomy explained, holding out his hands to show the length. 'It's eighteen inches, maybe two foot long. He keeps it on his right side, in his trousers.'

'How come,' Thomas asked, 'you are telling me this?'

Coomy's bluish lips parted in a narrow smile.

'Well?'

'I don't like Jason much,' Coomy said.

'That's not enough of a reason. There are a lot of other men here who have better reason to dislike him. At least he lets you near the pot where there's still meat in it.'

'For now,' Coomy told him, 'you'll have to accept the explanation I just gave you.' And he pushed himself away from the wall and started to walk away. Then he stopped and came back. 'There's something else I think you should know,' he said.

'I'm listening.'

'All of you are going to be moved out of here —'

'When?'

'Two days from now, possibly three.'

'Where are we going?'

'Rock Island,' Coomy answered.

Thomas' jaw went slack, and before he could ask how Coomy knew that, the man had turned and was already several paces away from him. Though he was on the verge of calling him back, Thomas couldn't bring himself to do it. But he continued to watch Coomy until he turned the corner of the barracks and was out of sight.

The yellow circle of the sun looked like an upended, polished twenty-dollar gold piece as it rested on the crown of a distant — and what appeared to be a somewhat higher — hilltop. Though Thomas had been given two very important pieces of information, he concentrated on the sun, and in a few minutes the lower segment of its arc vanished behind the top of the hill. A cold breeze suddenly sprang up, forcing him to turn up his collar and thrust his hands into his trouser pockets. Whatever warmth the sun had offered was gone. Thomas moved away from the wall and slowly made his way back to the entrance in the front of the barracks.

Regardless of what Jason might try to do now that he had reason to believe that Thomas had killed one of his own men, the real issue between them was the coat. Thomas was absolutely sure of that. Anything else was just so much sand in the eyes of the other men. Jason knew that as long as Thomas was alive and could challenge his right of ownership for the coat, he might lose it. And with winter fast coming on, Jason wanted to be certain that the coat would be his. The only way he could do that would be to provoke a fight with Thomas and, if not actually kill him, at least beat him into submission.

Once Thomas reached the front of the barracks the long twilight shadows already lay on the palisade and the area of the compound directly inside the front gate. He paused and looked up at the sky. It was a dark blue, but there were rain clouds to the south and east.

He shook his head, silently cursed the weather and then retreated inside the barracks and went directly to his pallet. As soon as he stretched out, Thomas felt as if every man in the room were looking at him.

After his first awareness of himself as the center of focus in the barracks, Thomas put his hands behind his head and stared up at the darkened ceiling. There was nothing he could do until Jason made the first move.

From what he could hear of the low talk between the men, most of them seemed more concerned about the impending transfer to Rock Island prison than anything else. Every southerner, in or out of uniform, knew about the infamous Northern prisons where unspeakable and unimaginable cruelties were meted out to Confederate soldiers. And of all the hells on earth, Rock Island's reputation was by far the worst.

Thomas almost gave a scornful laugh, not because he doubted for a moment that conditions in the Northern prisons were extremely harsh, but rather that exactly the same cruelties were practiced on Union troops in Confederate prisons. Hadn't he seen it with his own eyes when he visited his brother John in the Richmond prison?

Thomas shook his head and once again stared at the darkened ceiling. If he loved anyone other than Lisa, it was John. He could not even feel toward his own son Ethan the way he felt toward John. Often in the years he had fought, he had wondered what would have happened if he and John had been so luckless as to have met on the battlefield. The question was no longer of any importance, since both of them were now prisoners of war.

But as far as Thomas was concerned, he didn't intend to remain confined in a Northern prison, though not because his views were so ardently for the Confederacy and all it stood for. Those weren't his sentiments at all. He didn't hold with slavery, and as far as 'states' rights' went, he had been taught to believe the federal government.

He turned his head to look at the other men. Unlike them, he had joined the army not for any patriotic reason, but only to get away from his father and Helen … yes, even to be free of Lisa. Those were his reasons for fighting. Now they didn't seem to be worth the years of killing and privation he had endured, to say nothing of spending even more years in a Yankee prison.

But his resolve to escape did not stem from any new-found love for the principles of the Confederacy. Once he was free, Thomas had no intention of returning to the army — at least not right away, and perhaps never. His vision of the future did not go beyond the one possibility that had given him sustenance since his capture. That was to return home and kill his father. Whatever he would have to do to accomplish it he would do. It was a very clear and simple, purpose.

Thomas heaved a sigh and, closing his eyes, tried to imagine how his homecoming might be. But he did not get beyond remembering what the front yard and the house looked like, before someone said it was snowing.

Thomas opened his eyes and cursed aloud. The last thing the men needed was snow, and from their grumbling, it was obvious he read their feelings true, especially those whose shoes were in bad shape.

He swung himself into a sitting position, and was about to stand and go to the door to look at the snow, when he realized that Jason was coming toward him. His heart began to race.

He stood up and moved a pace away from his pallet, lest Jason make use of the wooden edge as a fulcrum. Even as the distance between the two men narrowed, the other men slipped off to either side, anxious to see what would happen. Jason held his pointed stick as if it were a sword. He walked slowly, and behind him were his half-dozen friends.

'Some 'un bring the lantern,' Jason ordered as he continued his relentless movement toward Thomas. 'I wanna 'ave light when I talks to the lootenant, and by t'e livin' Gward we gots lot to talk about, don't we, lootenant?'

Thomas made a quick step backward, grabbed hold of the thin blanket on the pallet, and in a moment was back to where he had previously been. He accomplished the movement with such rapidity that only when the men saw the blanket in his hand did they realize what had happened. And then they gasped with surprise.

Jason stopped.

'Where should I place the light?' one of his men asked.

Jason looked around.

'Hang it from the cross beam,' one of the men on the sidelines called out.

'That's not the only thin' it'd pleasure me ta hang,' Jason laughed.

Two men stepped out from the sidelines and, using their belts to support the lantern, suspended it from the low cross beam.

Jason nodded his head approvingly. 'I'd say that wuz a mighty fine job, an' I thankee,' he told them, and then, looking at Thomas, said, 'What say ya?'

Thomas glanced at the gently swinging lantern and then, focusing his eyes at Jason, said in a low, calm voice, 'I'd say you were a fool.'

'A fool!' Jason growled loudly. But the very next instant, he gave a forced laugh, and though he was not close enough for the point of his stick to reach Thomas, he playfully, thrust at the space between them.

The men made a low groaning sound as though they had felt the sharp tip against their bellies. But Thomas remained mute and motionless.

'We heared that ya kilt one of yer own men,' Jason said, waving his stick back and forth.

Thomas concentrated on the movement going on in front of him. His one hope of preventing Jason from skewering him would be to snare the stick in the folds of the blanket and then try to wrest it from him.

'Is that true?' Jason asked. 'The men wants to know.'

'Yeah,' several of the spectators on either side of the room chorused, 'we wants to know if'n ye kilt the man … one of yer own…'

Thomas glared at them and moving his head from one side and then to the other, he said, 'I have no reason to give an accounting of my actions to any of you.' He spoke with the authority of his rank. 'This fight between us,' he continued, facing Jason, 'would have come to be whether I killed a man or not.'

The men moved uneasily where they stood, making the rough wooden floor boards squeak under the changing weight. And for several moments nothing more was said. But then one of the men — Thomas couldn't tell who he was, because the voice came from somewhere along the side wall off to his right — demanded to know why he and Jason would have fought.

'Tell them, Jason,' Thomas said quickly.

'He's jest given ya a fancy line of talk,' Jason answered. The question took him by surprise and he stopped waving his stick.

'It were him that kilt the man, now ya ask him why he did that. Go ahead, ask him.'

No one did, but Thomas could see the faces of those men caught in the yellow circle of the light turn toward him questioningly.

'He needed killing,' Thomas said flatly.

'Ya were judge and jury!' a man called out.

'Yes,' Thomas answered, and added, 'his executioner too.'

Except for the sound of the men's hard breathing, the room was again quiet.

'I say he kilt the man —'

'Jason,' still another man called, 'ya ain't answered the lootenant.'

'Nothin' ta answer,' Jason said, beginning to wave his stick again. 'He told ya all that he kilt a sojer, a Confederit sojer.' He shook his head. 'Any man does that must be a damn Yankee lover. Why yer in this war, lootenant? Maybe ya should be with the blue-bellies?' And with that he lunged fiercely at Thomas' right shoulder. This time, by making a quick leap forward, he closed the distance between the tip of his stick and his opponent.

The point went through Thomas' tunic and into the flesh, and only by twisting to the left was he able to avoid receiving a deeper wound. The sudden pain flashed through his arm. The warm blood trickled down his sleeve and he struggled to hold on to the blanket. Thomas' vision blurred, and he had to shake his head in order to bring Jason back in focus.

'He don't look so good,' Jason said, beginning to weave from side to side. 'I bet the man 'e kilt never had a chance.' He lunged again, but this time he missed his mark. Jason laughed and continued to feint at his enemy.

Thomas watched him very carefully. As long as Jason held the stick, he had the advantage. He could always keep him out of reach. Then suddenly Thomas realized he might be able to get inside the length of the stick. If he could do that —

He began to circle Jason, first moving with the greatest radius between them.

'Look at him dance!' Jason exclaimed, to the amusement of the other men. 'All he needs is a fiddle.'

A burst of gruff laughter followed.

Thomas continued to circle, but the third time he moved around Jason, he lessened the distance between them.

Jason thrust at him again and found his mark. But Thomas had folded the blanket into an effective shield. The hit, had it gone all the way home, would have lodged the point in the man's gut and that would have been an end to it.

'Gwad damn ya te hell,' Jason shouted, 'stand still an' fight like a man!'

Thomas made no reply, but he maintained his movement. Even in the yellow light from the lantern suspended from the beam, he could see the sweat on Jason's face. And though he never once looked at the men who were watching, he sensed they were becoming more and more uneasy with each passing moment. He could hear them shuffling, coughing and even chortling nervously.

Time and time again Jason attempted to drive the point of his stick into the man, but he couldn't get a good fix on him, and when he did, the blanket got in the way.

Five minutes passed — maybe more, and still Thomas continued to circle his adversary. He soon realized that Jason's thrusts weren't as strong as they had been in the beginning, which could have meant that he was tiring or conserving his strength.

'Ya must'a kilt that man by runnin' him ta death,' Jason wheezed, and for an instant he paused, dropped the point of the stick and started to wipe his brow.

Thomas acted instinctively. He threw the blanket at the stick, pushing its point still more to the floor. Almost at the same time, he sprang directly at Jason and, bringing his knee up, smashed it into the man's groin.

Jason groaned, dropped his stick and staggered backward.

Thomas heard the men yell. Some of them screamed for blood, caring not whose it was, while others just shouted like animals. He paid no attention to the noise and hurled himself on Jason.

But this time, he sent his fist smashing into the man's face. Blood gushed from Jason's nose and again he staggered backward. Thomas went after him. His blood was up and he couldn't stop himself. He drove his fist into Jason's stomach and when the man doubled up, Thomas struck him in the face with his knee.

Jason thudded to the floor and tried to get away. But Thomas pulled him back and pounded his head against the wooden floor until the man screamed to be let go.

Breathing hard, Thomas took hold of the stick, and as he shouted, 'An eye for an eye,' he drove it through his own coat and into Jason's right shoulder. When he pulled it free, blood followed it.

Straddling him, Thomas battered his fists against Jason's head. There was more pleasure in —

'He's goin' to kill him!' someone shouted.

The words caught hold of Thomas' arms and stopped them. He leaped up and grabbed hold of the bloody stick, holding it at Jason's throat. He desperately wanted to push it into the jugular vein. God how he wanted to do it! He even started to exert pressure on his weapon, making the skin on the man's throat give way under the point…

'Don't do it, lieutenant!' Mr Coomy called out. 'He has had enough … more than enough.'

'The bastard should die!' Thomas answered. 'He killed three good men to get at me.'

'Who killed them?'

'Zeb!' Thomas shouted. 'Zeb!'

The men fell silent.

'That's not Zeb,' Mr Coomy told him, making his way out of the shadows to the light. 'That's only Jason.'

'Jason?' Thomas asked.

'Yes, Jason,' Mr Coomy said, leading Thomas away.

Thomas stopped and ran his sleeve over his eyes. 'For a few moments I thought he was someone else,' he explained in a low voice. He looked back at Jason. 'Is he hurt bad?'

'Some.'

'I didn't go looking for him,' Thomas said. 'I would have waited awhile before — Not that it matters much, since we were both spoiling for a fight.'

Coomy agreed.

'Would you do me a favor?' Thomas asked as he watched some of the men drag Jason to his pallet near the door.

Coomy nodded.

'Pass the word that there'll be no special line-up at the pot tomorrow or any other time.'

'Yes, lieutenant!' From the snap in the man's answer, Thomas almost expected him to salute. But instead Mr Coomy suggested that he get some sleep.

'Never did get to see the snow,' Thomas said, pointing toward the door with the blood-tipped stick.

'It will be there in the morning,' Mr Coomy told him.

He nodded and went toward his pallet. Before reaching it, he turned, looked up at the lantern and shook his head. Then he flung himself down on the wooden boards, and minutes later was asleep.

During the night, Thomas sensed that someone was near him. He bolted up in time to see a shadow dart away. But when he lowered his eyes, he saw his coat neatly folded at the foot of his pallet.

THREE

There was snow on the ground the next morning and it was deep, especially along the east and south walls of the palisade, where there were high wind-sculptured drifts. Thomas stood at the barracks door and scanned the sky for some indication that the storm was moving off. But the clouds were an ugly gray.

'Think it'll stop, sir?'

'Hardly,' Thomas answered, without bothering to turn around and look at the man who spoke. 'At least not until late afternoon — maybe even not then,' he added.

'Be powerful mean ta travel in this kinda weather.'

Thomas nodded.

'Sir, ya think the Yankees will move us today?'

Thomas had all but forgotten about the move from where they were to the prison at Rock Island. 'I don't rightly know,' he answered, shaking his head. Then suddenly he realized that he had been addressed as 'Sir.' He turned to look at the man, but to his surprise the man was a boy, possibly no more than seventeen. He was average-sized, had brown hair and hazel eyes. If it were not for the fact that he was wearing a uniform, he would have looked like any other boy of his age. No, that wasn't true. This boy was God awful thin, and when Thomas saw that the boy wasn't wearing any shoes, he understood his concern about the snow.

''Scuse me, sir, but I didn't mean te trouble ya none,' the boy said, flushing under Thomas' stare. And he drew himself up to stand at attention, saluted, did an about face and immediately went to his bunk.

After Thomas returned the salute, though not in time for the boy to see it, he remained at the door awhile longer and wondered if indeed the Yankees would move them in such weather. If that did happen, he was certain that if they were marched for even a short distance most of the men without boots or shoes wouldn't be able to make it. Those who didn't die along the way would lose their feet from frostbite and the gangrene that would follow. Even some of those men who would survive would be crippled for the rest of their lives.

He shrugged and, with that simple gesture, stopped thinking about the possible consequences to the men and concerned himself with his chance for survival. He looked down at his boots and was confident that they would last until — until he escaped.

Thomas turned and went back to his pallet, where, leaning against the rough log wall, he thought about how the boy had saluted him. He found it peculiar, even humorous enough to make him smile.

The remainder of the morning passed slowly. But now and then one of the men would go to the door, look out and utter a curse. Then someone announced that the blue-bellies were coming into the compound with food.

Almost as a single man, those prisoners who could got to their feet. Thomas expected them to run pell-mell for the pot. But no one moved. It took him a few moments to understand that the men were waiting for him to go first, or tell them that they could go. Either way, they were, by their actions, acknowledging him as their commanding officer.

Suddenly he saw Mr Coomy coming toward him. 'Good God,' he said when the man was within earshot of a whisper. 'What the hell am I going to do?'

'What they want you to,' Mr Coomy responded, with more than a hint of a smile on his lips.

'But why?'

'You know the old saying: "To the victor belongs the spoils."'

Thomas didn't know what the hell Coomy was talking about. But he wasn't about to stand there and palaver with him while the men were waiting to go to the pot. 'We'll talk later,' he told Coomy, and then, walking out into the middle of the room, asked for a sergeant.

A man stepped forward and presented himself with a salute as 'Sergeant Stanford Hawkins'.

He returned the salute and said, 'Sergeant, take the men to the pot.'

'Yes sir!' the man responded, and immediately ordered the men to form a column of twos.

'Why aren't all of the men going?' Thomas asked, when he saw some of them were still on their pallets.

'Some haven't shoes,' the sergeant answered, 'some is too sick.'

Thomas nodded. 'By my count,' he said, 'there are fifteen men here.'

The sergeant looked at him questioningly.

'The first fifteen men who finish at the pot will bring back rations for the men who remained here.'

'But the blue-belly cook —'

'Tell him those were my orders.'

'Yes, sir!'

They saluted each other, and Thomas waited until the sergeant marched the men out of the barracks before he returned to where Coomy was standing.

'I'd say,' the civilian told him with a broad grin, 'you handled that right smartly.'

Thomas didn't answer. He was trying to understand why he foolishly went further than called for. It would have been sufficient to order the men to be marched out to the pot. No one else seemed concerned about the men who could not go out of the barracks. Why should he have taken it upon himself to see that they would be fed?

No sooner had he posed these questions to himself than Thomas' thoughts moved swiftly off in a different direction, and as he looked at Coomy, he had the peculiar feeling that the man held more than a slight rein on the events of the last twelve to fifteen hours. Maybe he was responsible for getting Jason fired up enough to fight by telling him about Zeb —

'Something bothering you?' Mr Coomy asked, watching the expression on the lieutenant's face, and in his eyes, change from moment to moment as he attempted to examine the facts, such as he might understand them.

'I don't want to command them,' Thomas said after a long pause. 'I'll be lucky if I can take care of myself.'

'That's hardly the point,' Mr Coomy said. 'Once you went to the center of the room and issued orders, you accepted them.'

Thomas shook his head.

Mr Coomy smiled and asked, 'Then why did you fight Jason?'

'Because he wouldn't have been satisfied with anything less,' Thomas answered.

'Only that?'

'All right,' Thomas said in a low angry voice, 'all right, I fought him because I wanted my coat back.'

Coomy's jaw went slack and for a few moments he said nothing.

'He took what belonged to me —'

'I don't believe you!'

Thomas shrugged and said, 'I don't care what you believe … when a man pushes me, I push back.'

'I knew that the first time I saw you,' Mr Coomy laughed. 'The fact of the matter is, I knew that soon after I had heard what took place between you and Captain Walsh.'

Thomas cocked his head to one side and looked at him questioningly.

'When I saw that the back of your head had been laid open,' Mr Coomy explained with a smile, 'I became curious.'

'I don't like people poking around in my business,' Thomas told him sharply.

'Listen,' he said, putting his hand on Thomas' arm, 'before you go off in a huff … I've been waiting six long weeks for someone like you to show up. At first I thought Jason might be the man, but I soon discovered that he was a bag of wind and not very brave —'

'Slow down some,' Thomas told him, realizing that there was more than fever burning Coomy's eyes now. 'Tell me why you were waiting for someone like me.'

Mr Coomy nodded and began to laugh. Then he went into a fit of coughing, and finally he spit blood. But when he calmed down enough to speak, he said, 'To escape, Lieutenant Thomas Carey. To escape and spill Yankee blood all over the land. That's why I've been waiting for someone like you. That's why!'

The man was wild-looking, but what he had just said quickened the beat of Thomas' heart. He was more certain than ever that Coomy had pushed Jason into the fight by telling him about Zeb. And Thomas guessed that Coomy knew why he had fought and had killed Zeb.

'What do you say to that?' Mr Coomy questioned, his voice tight with emotion.

Thomas was about to answer that he would go his own way when the time came, but he checked himself and said instead, 'It can't be done from here, if that's what you're thinking.'

'I've watched you examine the place,' Mr Coomy told him with obvious admiration, 'and I know that if anyone could have gotten out from the compound, you would have.'

Ignoring the compliment, Thomas asked, 'From where, then?'

'I want to be sure of my man before I say one word more,' Mr Coomy replied, shaking his head. 'Will you take command of the men?'

The man was playing him and Thomas didn't like it. Being beholden to him was one thing, and Thomas would have been more than willing to pay him back when the time came, but Mr Coomy was trying to ride him.

'Listen,' Thomas said, suddenly reaching out and grabbing hold of Coomy by the front of his shirt, 'I've had enough of this cat-and-mouse gaming. Who are you?'

'Let go of me!' Mr Coomy hissed. His eyes bulged out of their deep sockets and his sallow complexion took on a reddish hue.

Thomas shook his head.

'I'm a Confederate sympathizer,' Mr Coomy said brittlely. He hated Thomas for being physically stronger than himself.

'Spy?'

'I do whatever I can to help the Southern cause,' he answered, breathing hard.

Thomas nodded and released him. He knew that each side had its sympathizers in the territory of the other, and here, along the Chickahominy where the two great armies faced each other, such men would be important sources of information. Just by looking at a man in civilian clothes there was no way of knowing whether he favored the South or the North. Even the way a man spoke didn't necessarily indicate where his sympathies lay.

'How come you're here?' he asked.

'I lost my way and wandered into a restricted area,' Mr Coomy explained, smoothing out the front of his shirt.

Thomas chuckled and said, 'That's a likely story.'

'I could hardly say anything else under the circumstances.'

'Okay,' Thomas said with a nod, 'that answers one question. Now what about the escape?'

Mr Coomy took a deep breath, and when he finished wheezing it out of his lungs, he said, 'The prisoners are marched from here some thirty miles north to where the railroad is, where they're loaded on trains that take —'

'Thirty miles!' Thomas exclaimed. He took a quick look at the men who were in the barracks and shook his head. 'They'll never make it,' he whispered. His eyes came back to Coomy. 'A thirty-mile march in snow would be hard enough for a strong man to endure, but for a man with the lung disease —'

'Don't worry about me,' he said, looking straight at Thomas. 'I'll make it, and if I don't you and the others will … that's what's important.'

'What others?' Thomas asked. 'I thought that we were the only ones who would try to escape.'

Mr Coomy shook his head and said, 'As many as possible. That's why I want you to take command now. It will avoid trouble later.'

'It will be harder to move with more men than fewer.'

'As many as possible,' Mr Coomy maintained adamantly.

Thomas was not about to argue the point — at least not for the time being. But he did realize that the man, like so many other patriotic men he had known, couldn't see the forest for the trees: it was one thing to be a soldier and fight the enemy, but it was something else again to be a band of marauders behind the enemy lines.

'Go on,' he said, 'tell me the rest of your scheme.'

'There is one guard for every five men, which means for a group this size there will be twelve men assigned. I have people on the outside who have been watching the compound. They'll know when we move. Half way to the railhead we pass through a gorge. That's where they'll be waiting.'

'How many?' Thomas questioned.

'Enough to allow us to take care of the blue-bellies and make our escape.'

'What about mounts?'

'Three miles south of the gorge there's a farm,' Mr Coomy said. 'We'll find everything we need there.'

'Are you sure?' Thomas asked. The plan was deceptively simple. But its success depended completely on Coomy's friends.

'I'm sure.'

'It might work,' Thomas said with a nod. 'But a large group of men will leave a big trail in the snow.'

'Let's hope the good Lord sees fit to hide our tracks,' he said with a shrug. 'But even if He doesn't intercede on behalf of our just cause, it will be at least one full day before the people at the railhead begin to suspect that something has happened to the shipment of prisoners. By then we'll be miles away.'

What he said made sense, and Thomas realized that Mr Coomy had probably worked out the entire plan with his friends in the event that one of them might be taken prisoner for trespassing in a restricted area or violating some other military law.

'Now you know,' Mr Coomy said with a deep sigh. 'But you still have not answered me.'

Thomas rubbed his chin. He suspected that Coomy was using him, not only to control the men but also, once they were free, to give the men the feeling that they were still under military authority. If it ever came to a showdown between them, Thomas didn't doubt for a moment that Coomy would in some way manage to have him killed. He also faced the fact that Coomy's plan might be his only chance to get away, but at the same time Thomas realized that he might be forced to escape a second time, should Coomy make any attempt to stop him from returning to Texas.

He lowered his hand. There was no sense thinking about what might happen between them after the escape. Thomas decided that he would be foolish not to accept the offer, since he was sure that Mr Coomy would never cotton to the fact that Thomas was using him as much as — perhaps even more than — he thought he was using Thomas. That aspect of the arrangement made Thomas smile. 'All right,' he said, 'I agree.'

'Thank the good Lord!' Mr Coomy exclaimed, extending his hand.

'We'll see about that,' Thomas answered as he shook the man's hand. 'We'll see how much thanks he deserves.'

'I'm a man of faith … faith in our cause and in the Almighty.'

Thomas let go of Coomy's hand and, in a low voice, said, 'Then we might balance each other, since I don't have any faith.' And almost as an afterthought, he suggested that they go out to the pot and get something to eat.

Later that afternoon Sergeant Hawkins, a short, stocky man

with a large copper-colored mustache and sharp blue eyes, told Thomas in answer to his question that there were two other men among the prisoners who held a sergeant's rank. One of them was Jason and the other was named Louis Sands.

'Better fetch them,' Thomas told Hawkins.

The sergeant hesitated. 'Maybe, sir,' he suggested, 'it would be best to jest ask Sands.'

'I don't think so, sergeant,' Thomas replied and then informed the man that he had something important to tell them.

Hawkins started to salute.

'Sergeant,' Thomas said, 'I think we can get along without that.'

The man smiled and went off to round up the other two men, while Thomas returned to his pallet and waited to see what would happen.

Hawkins went straight to Sands, said a few words and pointed to Thomas. Then Sands stood up and walked slowly across the room. But when Hawkins went to Jason, he seemed to run into difficulty. Several times he looked at the lieutenant. Jason was obviously giving Hawkins some lip.

Thomas got to his feet and, in a loud voice, said, 'Sergeant Hawkins, tell that man to report to me immediately!'

In an instant it seemed as though every man in the barracks stopped breathing. For a few moments nothing happened. Then Jason slowly stood up and he began to walk. The sudden flare of tension eased. 'All right, men,' Thomas said, as soon as the three non-coms were at his pallet, 'we're going to start acting like soldiers again.'

'We're prisoners,' Jason said.

Thomas nodded. 'That's right, Jason,' he answered calmly. 'But that doesn't mean we can't act like soldiers and like men.'

Hawkins and Sands agreed, but Jason remained balky. The results of the beating Thomas had given him the night before were very much in evidence. His face was swollen and the wound in his shoulder was covered with dried blood. He looked even meaner than he had previously.

Thomas paid little heed to Jason's sulkiness. First he divided the remaining prisoners into three groups and placed a sergeant in charge of each. He told them that they would be responsible to see that each man under their command would be fed, whether or not the man could make it out to the pot.

'Don't see why we're playin' sojer,' Jason commented sourly, 'when in a day or two we're all goin' ta be sent ta Rock Islan'.'

That gave Thomas his opening and he said, 'That's just it, we're not going to Rock Island.' And before Jason or the other two sergeants could speak, he told them about the plan to escape. This information immediately changed Jason's attitude, and he listened carefully and without comment to what Thomas had to say. And finally Thomas said, 'Once we start for the farmhouse, the men must keep moving. That's why we have to act like soldiers. We can't have any stragglers.'

'What about the men wid'out shoes?' Hawkins asked.

'They'll wrap their feet in strips of blanket and whatever else is handy.'

'The sick an' the wounded,' Sands questioned, 'how will they make it?'

Thomas shook his head. 'I don't think they'll ever reach the gorge,' he said, 'at least not in this snow.'

'Wot happens after we get te the farm house?' Hawkins questioned.

Thomas hesitated and thought what his own situation would be at that time. Then he shrugged and said, 'Let's not take things too fast. First we have to get there.'

The three men laughed, and Hawkins assured him that they would do it.

'Now each of you,' Thomas explained, 'take the men in your group and tell them what I have told you. Explain to them that it's not going to be easy but once they overpower the guards they won't have to worry about getting shot. Every man, including those who are sick and wounded, must know what to expect and what to do. I'll leave it to you to decide which of the men take care of the guards. Do any of you have any questions?'

'Jest one, lootenant,' Jason said.

'Go ahead,' Thomas answered, 'ask it.'

'Is this *yer* plan?'

The question took Thomas by surprise. He wasn't sure how the men would react if he told them the truth, but at the same time he saw no reason to lie to them. 'Let's say,' he answered, striking a compromise between what was true and false, 'that it's a kind of joint action.'

Jason gave a lopsided smile and looked toward Coomy, who sat on his pallet watching the meeting.

Thomas expected Jason to say something else, but the man kept silent. A few minutes later the three sergeants were deeply involved in the task of briefing the men, while Thomas stretched out on his pallet. The meeting had gone much better than he had expected. Hawkins and Sands would do what they had to, when the time came, though it was obvious to him that Hawkins was the better non-com of the two. If anything bothered him, it was how quickly and easily Jason's attitude had changed once he was told about the escape. There was no doubt that the man had shrewdly guessed whose plan it really was, and Thomas wondered how much more Jason could figure out. If it occurred to Jason how he had been used by

Coomy, then he might cause a great deal of trouble somewhere along the way, or later when they reached the farmhouse … *if* they reached the farmhouse. Like Hawkins, Thomas was sure they would reach their goal. But it was what would happen afterward that he found worrisome.

After a while he stopped fretting, and closing his eyes he enjoyed the luxury of thinking about how he would open the front door of his house and what the expression on his father's face would be when they came face to face. That would surely be a sight worth waiting for.

Gradually Thomas felt himself relaxing. His breathing became slow and regular as he drifted off into a light sleep. But after what seemed like an incredibly short time, the low boom of thunder rolled toward him from far away. Big dark balls of it crashed against the fragile shell of sleep. The explosions of thunder quickened.

In a futile attempt to rid himself of the tormenting booms, Thomas moved his head from side to side. Then suddenly the true nature of the sound registered, and he bolted upwards. Though the barracks was dark, Thomas sensed the men around him were awake and tense.

Several moments passed before the deep-throated thunder of another explosion rolled through the night. Thomas strained his whole body toward the sound. Three more explosions followed, in rapid succession of each other.

'Ours or theirs?' a man close by asked.

'Sounds like ours,' Thomas answered, leaving his pallet and walking quickly to the door.

The snow had stopped, and the bright white light from a half-moon turned the drifts of snow into mounds of silver.

Thomas turned his attention toward the south, hoping to catch sight of the distant flash of cannon fire. The night was too bright, and the top of the palisade too high, for him to see anything more than moonlit sky.

Hawkins came up alongside him and peered out into the night. 'Maybe,' the sergeant suggested after a few moments, 'it's jest to reset their guns?'

'That wouldn't take continuous fire,' Thomas answered.

'Sir,' Hawkins said, 'lookee thar, the blue-bellies are openin' the gate.'

But Thomas had already seen what was happening and guessed what was about to happen. 'Tell Sands and Jason to get the men ready to march,' he said, without turning to look at Hawkins.

'Now, sir?'

'That's an order, sergeant!' Thomas answered, as he watched the twelve Yankee soldiers slowly plow their way through the snow that lay between the gate and the barracks. 'We're moving out ahead of time.'

'Wot about the plan?'

'We won't know about that,' he said, shaking his head, 'until we reach the gorge. Now get the men ready.'

'Yes, sir!'

Thomas nodded and turned toward the open door. As he watched the progress of the Yankee soldiers through the snow, he almost wished he had some of Coomy's faith in the cause for which all of the prisoners were about to suffer; and for the God who would not only allow them to suffer, but would look kindly on it when each man's time came to stand before Him.

Thomas snorted at his own thoughts, and a moment later moved back into the barracks to wait for the blue-bellies.

FOUR

The clear air was so intensely cold and crisp that the men who stood in front of the barracks found it absolutely necessary to stamp their feet and wave their arms in order to prevent them from becoming numb. And in the distance the sound of cannonading could still be heard, though the frequency of the explosions had become more irregular.

Thomas was at one end of the front rank and Coomy was next to him. Their attention was focused on the mounted Union officer who came to an abrupt halt directly in front of the first rank after a short gallop through the heavy snow from the gate.

'You prisoners are being moved to a railhead, and then from there to Rock Island,' the mounted lieutenant announced. 'We will stop five minutes out of every hour. There will be one five-hour halt for sleep at dawn tomorrow. Straggling will not be tolerated. Every man who is capable of walking will stay in the line of march. Every second hour a head count will be made. For every man who escapes a man will be shot —'

An angry murmur of disapproval arose from the men.

'Silence!' the lieutenant ordered, riding his brown, steam-breathing horse up and down in front of the prisoners. 'That's much better.' He rode up to Mr Coomy and said, 'You there, sir, step out of line.'

Coomy was about to step forward, but Thomas grabbed hold of his arm and held him in the line.

'Release that man,' the lieutenant ordered. 'He is not going with the rest of you.'

Thomas stepped forward. 'Sir,' he said, 'I am in command of these men —'

'Is that so?' the lieutenant answered, and in a matter of moments he crowded his mount so close to Thomas that he was forced to fall back into the line of prisoners. 'You are not in command of anything,' the Union officer said, after he guided his horse back a few steps. 'Mr Coomy is to be executed —'

The prisoners started to move forward.

'Guards,' the lieutenant shouted, 'shoot the first man who takes another step.'

The Union troop slapped their rifles to the ready.

'Halt!' Thomas ordered. 'Stand easy, men. Fall back into line.'

For a few moments they hesitated, but then obeyed.

'Now, Mr Coomy,' the lieutenant said, 'will you step forward.'

Coomy turned to Thomas and whispered, 'Follow the plan!' Then straightening his shoulders, he walked forward.

'Sergeant,' the Union officer said, 'carry out the execution.'

Thomas and the other prisoners watched the Union soldiers march Coomy to the wall, stand him against it, fall back ten paces, turn and, at the sergeant's order, lift their rifles.

The lieutenant glanced over his shoulder. 'Get it done with, sergeant,' he called.

'Yessir,' the man answered and a moment later ordered, 'Fire!'

Sounding as one, six shots rang out.

Coomy's body jerked up, almost off the ground, then sagged against the wall and pitched forward into the snow. To be sure that he was dead, the sergeant bent over him, rolled him over and then, drawing his revolver, shot him in the head.

Even as the sharp smell of burnt powder floated across the front of the compound, the lieutenant was already ordering the guards to take up their positions and the march to the railhead began.

Thomas stayed at the front of the column. He made no attempt to think about Coomy's execution, except to realize that had Coomy been a Union sympathizer in a Confederate prison, he would have met the same fate, and probably sooner. He heaved a deep sigh and hoped that Coomy's friends were watching the prison compound.

Once the column was beyond the palisade, Thomas saw the distant flashes of the cannon. He could tell from the frenzied activity in the Yankee camp as they passed through it that General Lee must have ordered the units on the Chickahominy to attack. Whether the action was just a feint in this particular sector or part of an all-out action, Thomas couldn't begin to guess. But it was obvious that the Yankees weren't taking any chances, and were sending men and materiel toward the sound of the cannonading.

As soon as the prisoners were out of sight of the bivouac area, the march began in earnest. The lieutenant kept up a grueling pace, and in less than an hour some of the wounded and sick began to lag. Three dropped in the snow and were left there to die.

Thomas knew that by morning none of the sick and wounded would be with the column. But there was nothing he could do to save them. His main concern was to get as many men as possible to the gorge and then to the farmhouse.

During the first head count, he moved back along the column and told each of his sergeants that the plan remained the same, that they were not to stop for a man who fell out of the line of march and to try to stop any man who might try to escape. Hawkins and Sands took his commands without questioning them. But Jason gave him trouble.

'More of us will die,' Jason told him, 'than will make it.'

Thomas nodded.

'There's enough of us ta take them,' he said.

'No,' Thomas answered. 'Our only chance is to wait until we get to the gorge.'

Jason glowered at him. 'Wot makes ya so sure the men will be there?' he asked.

'For all our sakes,' Thomas said, 'let's hope they'll be there.' And then he went back to the head of the column and the march began again.

The night finally dissolved in an agony of cold. Even though Thomas had a coat and a good pair of boots, his body was numb. Behind him he heard the low moans of men who lacked a coat or shoes or both.

Finally the lieutenant called a halt. 'You have five hours,' he told the prisoners, 'and then we move on.'

Thomas approached the Union officer and asked permission to build fires for his men.

The lieutenant dismounted and gave his horse over to the care of one of the guards. 'I cannot even permit that luxury to my own troops. Your men will have to make the best of conditions,' he said to Thomas.

'There are no conditions to make the best of,' Thomas said in a low calm voice. Up to that moment, he had not paid any attention to the lieutenant. To him, he was just another Yankee officer. But now as they stood eye to eye, Thomas could not escape looking at him. He was about his height, but he had blond hair and pale blue eyes. Thomas guessed he was probably popular with the ladies.

'You rebs,' the lieutenant said, 'should have thought about that before you decided to go to war.'

Thomas nodded. 'I suppose you're right,' he answered. 'But they're not fighting now.' And he gestured toward the men. 'They're just cold, hungry and tired.'

The lieutenant seemed to hesitate, but then he shrugged his shoulders and said, 'I have my orders. I'm sure that you understand my position.'

'Just one fire, then,' Thomas asked. 'That will let the men take turns at it.'

'If I allow one,' the officer said, 'then I might as well allow several, and I cannot do that.'

Thomas glanced quickly from one side to the other and back to the lieutenant. He knew that he could probably grab and kill him with the short end of the stick he had taken from Jason after the fight. Maybe some of the men would be able to overcome a few of the guards, but enough of them would be left to shoot all if not every one of the prisoners.

'I hope you just don't intend to stand there and stare at me,' the lieutenant said.

Thomas blinked, shook his head and brought himself back to the reality of the moment.

'Then I suggest that you too get some rest.'

'Yes,' Thomas answered, 'that's what I intend to do.' And, turning, he went to re-join his men. But before he stretched out on the snow, he went from group to group urging them to continue the march when it began again.

In one group he saw the boy who had spoken to him after his fight with Jason. The boy's feet were very red. Two men were rubbing them. Thomas bent close to the boy and asked him if he thought he would be able to keep going, once they started again.

The boy raised his head and, tears streaming down his cheeks, said, 'Not likely, sir.' And then he lowered his head.

Thomas reached out and was just about to touch him when he stopped himself. To show that he felt anything toward one man — even if the man was a boy — might be taken by the others as a sign of weakness, and what they needed was a show of strength. There were other men who were without shoes, and whose feet were raw and bleeding, just as this boy's were. He did not, and could not, have compassion for all of them.

'You'll make it,' Thomas told the boy. 'We'll all make it.'

'Yes, sir,' the youth answered.

Thomas finally sat down in the snow. Leaning his back against the trunk of an oak tree, he drew his feet up and used them to support his arms, on which he rested his head. Now that he had taken time to rest, he became very aware of his own weariness. Never had he been so tired, so hungry, and so very cold. The realization that he was cold made him feel even colder, and he started to shiver.

He raised his head and looked at the other men. All of them were trembling. Some were openly moaning, especially those who were shoeless. Thomas shook his head and then lowered it again. Of all the men he had known, these God-forgotten soldiers were by far the bravest. He had no doubt that if there was a hell in the life to come, that it wasn't — as men of the cloth preached — full of fire and burning brimstone, but was bitter cold with a never-ending wind-driven snow. *That* was hell. Anything else would be too comfortable for eternal damnation.

He looked at the men again, but this time his eyes moved from individual to individual as he tried to make an appraisal of each man's chance to survive. When he finished, he came to the conclusion that with some luck thirty-five, maybe forty out of the original sixty would make it to the gorge, and of that number only about twenty would be in any condition to fight. The odds against a successful mass escape would mount with each remaining hour between now and the time it took them to reach the gorge. And as this happened, his own chance for freedom would also be whittled away.

Thomas gritted his teeth. He could not allow that to happen. He must escape. He took a deep breath and, exhaling, sent a cloud of steam rushing from his nostrils. To his way of thinking, none of the men had a reason as powerful as his own. Though they were all suffering, only Thomas knew what it felt like to burn with hate. No man with him would ever know how much he wanted to live in order to kill his father. The very thought of it sent a thrilling surge of warmth through him which, for a few moments, allowed Thomas to stop shivering…

There was a strange heat in the knowledge that his father had tried to have him killed. There were reasons that Thomas could think of: the old man loved his daughter-in-law more than he loved his son; the old man had a grandson to whom he could give the land; the old man hated him; the old man was crazy; the old man had taken it in his hands to do the work of an avenging God. How like the Bible-believing son-of-a-bitch that would have been.

He remembered that time after he and Helen had argued loudly and violently…

'I want to talk to you,' his father had said, catching up to Thomas before he was halfway across the yard.

'What about?' Thomas asked, continuing to walk.

'I think you know,' William said.

'I don't want to —'

'Will you stop!' William exclaimed. He was rapidly losing patience with Thomas and his son's abuse of Helen was hurrying his feelings along.

'There's nothing to talk about,' Thomas answered, meeting the old man's steely eyes without flinching.

'She's a good woman,' William said. 'Better than you deserve.'

'In your eyes,' Thomas told him. 'But hardly in bed.'

'Is that all you think about?'

Thomas shook his head. 'No,' he replied. 'Sometimes I think how damn foolish I was not to have hightailed it out of here when I had the chance.'

'Have you been seeing that woman in Paso Diablo?' William growled.

'What I do or don't do, father, is none of your damn business,' Thomas answered flatly. 'And what's more,' he added, 'don't make it any of your business.'

'Is that a warning?'

Thomas shrugged. 'You wanted me married, so I'm married,' he said. 'For better or for worse, eh? Well, let me tell you, Father, it was for the worse. Not that you really care. You got yourself a Bible-reading, Bible-believing daughter-in-law out of it. But I didn't get a thing..'

'Are you blaming her for what happened?'

Thomas shook his head. 'I blame myself,' he said sharply. 'I took my gun off to get married —'

'Women and killing are all you ever think about.'

'You forgot whiskey, father,' Thomas told him. 'The best trio a man ever had: Women, whiskey, and fighting. Now leave me be. I had enough for one morning.'

Thomas shook his head. None of these things seemed to warrant sending Zeb after him. But Zeb had come, and sooner or later Thomas would go back and —

'Lootenant?'

Thomas looked up and saw Hawkins, Sands and Jason standing almost in front of him. He had been so involved with his own thoughts that he had not seen them approach.

Hawkins called him again and added, 'We come ta talk with you, sir.'

Thomas scrambled to his feet with the uncomfortable feeling that the men knew he would not hesitate to sacrifice them, as well as all the others, to gain his own freedom.

'Ain't going ta have enough men ta make it,' Jason said, stepping forward from the others, 'when we gets ta the gorge.'

'That's a fact, sir,' Hawkins commented with a nod.

Thomas looked at Sands.

'I think we should try,' Sands said.

'The men don't have no strength now,' Jason said. 'They're goin' ta have less when we reach the gorge.'

Thomas shook his head. He didn't blame the men for their attitude. If he were in their position, he would probably feel the same way. To them the risk was no longer worth the effort. But he couldn't settle for the alternative. There was no guarantee that he — or, for that matter, any of them — would survive the years at Rock Island.

'You men,' he said, 'are free to do what you want.'

The three sergeants looked questioningly at each other and then at him.

'I'll put it to you this way,' Thomas said, 'once the shooting starts, you or your men don't have to do anything.'

'But what will you do?' Sands asked.

'Try and kill the lieutenant,' Thomas answered flatly, 'and then make for the farmhouse.'

Sands nodded. 'Like I said,' he announced, 'I'll try.'

'What about you, Hawkins?' Thomas asked.

'Well, maybe some will get away. I'll stick with it.'

'And you, Jason?' Thomas questioned.

Jason rubbed his beard and was about to answer when from down the road came the sound of galloping horses. Moments later a troop of Union cavalry came rushing toward them.

The captain in charge of the troop slowed down long enough to shout to the lieutenant that the Confederates had breached the line and that the 'whole damn division was falling back'.

The prisoners began to cheer.

'If I were you,' the captain yelled to the lieutenant, 'I'd get these bastards moving before they become part of the rebel army again.' And then he galloped off, sending a shower of snow over the prisoners on both sides of the road.

The lieutenant lost no time in following the captain's advice, and within minutes the march was resumed. But before the column reformed, Jason assured Thomas that he, and what would be left of his men, would do what had to be done when they reached the gorge.

The pace was quickened. The hourly halt was abandoned, though the lieutenant paused briefly every second hour to take a head count.

Many times during the morning the column was forced off the road to make way for a variety of Union troops who were moving along the same road. Whole detachments of cavalry galloped by, followed by horse-drawn artillery and caissons. There were even infantry units of regimental strength moving in the same general direction as the prisoners. And lastly came the slow-moving ambulances, and from the number of wounded it was obvious to Thomas, and any of the other men who were still aware of something other than their own misery, that a battle had taken place and the blue-bellies had caught the worst of it.

Thomas first realized the magnitude of the Confederate success when he saw the ambulances, and he hoped that the confusion of the Union forces would be an unexpected aid to him and his men. If they could successfully overpower the guards and make for the farmhouse, the blue-bellies might think that the lieutenant and the guards were killed by a force of Confederate Cavalry. There was also the possibility that they might be overtaken by the pursuing Confederates. But that, Thomas realized, was unlikely, since the Yankees were bound to fight some sort of rear guard action.

By mid-morning, the flow of Union troops dwindled to a mere trickle. And Thomas could only guess whether that meant the Confederate advance had been halted, or the troops had been pulled back, or even that the Union forces had taken the initiative away from Lee's men. Of course, there was also the possibility that the action had shifted to a different sector along the Chickahominy.

As the march continued into the early afternoon, all of the sick and wounded had fallen out of the column and were left to die. And half the number of men without shoes or boots met the same fate. Once a man, wherever he was in the column, dropped out and fell into the snow, he was left where he had fallen. No one in front or behind him said a word or made any effort to help. All that happened was that the next man in the column quickened his step to fill the empty place.

No matter how fast the column moved, it never seemed fast enough for the lieutenant. At first he used words and threats to get the prisoners to increase their pace, but when this had no effect, he ordered the guards to prod the men with their rifles. For a while the men in the column responded, but then the weak sun vanished behind a milky cloud cover and the wind picked up just enough to blow snow against the faces of the men.

Much to the lieutenant's consternation, they slowed down again.

'By the living God,' he swore, 'either you bastards quicken your pace or I'll —' He stopped, reined in his mount and, standing in the stirrups, ordered his men to fix bayonets. 'Now we'll see whether or not you sons-of-bitches move. Any reb who doesn't,' he told his men, 'prod him along with the bayonet.'

Other than making him spit with disgust, the lieutenant's order meant nothing to Thomas, whose thoughts were almost wholly centered on the possibility that it might snow again. In fact, from the look of the sky and the bite of the wind, he was almost positive that it would. But the question of when it would start was important now. If it began before they reached the gorge, Coomy's friends might not be able to draw a bead on their targets, and then the men would have to kill all of the guards. There seemed to be damn slim chance of that happening. But on the other hand, if it snowed after they escaped it would cover their tracks to the farmhouse.

The light began to wane, but whether it was because of the late hour or a thickening of the clouds or a combination of both conditions, Thomas didn't know and cared significantly less. He too was beginning to feel the effects of the long hours of cold, hunger and fatigue. Even the wound in his shoulder bothered him more than it had before. He no longer kept his head up, but looked down at the snow, trying to take advantage of the furrows made earlier by the Union troops who had passed that way. It took practically all his will power to keep his legs moving, and even he began to doubt that any one of them would have sufficient strength to overpower the guard detachment and go another few miles cross country to the farmhouse. But each time his resolve to care flagged somewhat, it was quickly given grim determination when he remembered his purpose.

By the last head count the column had been reduced to forty men, and Thomas was certain that several more men would drop out before they reached the gorge. There might have been a chance of all forty of them reaching the gorge, but it had begun to snow again. Thomas couldn't help but feel that if their cause — as Coomy and so many others claimed — was right, and if — as these same people said — the Almighty was on their side, then He was sure taking one helluva way to show it.

Thomas shook his head and continued to walk hunched down in the huge collar of his coat. It took him some time to realize that the snow through which he plodded had not been trodden on by anything more than the lieutenant's horse, which was in front of him by no more than two paces. This meant that the Union troops he had seen earlier had left the road some distance back. He wondered whether they had cut north to establish a new line or swung south to counter-attack? Visualizing the consequences of each movement gave him something to think about that took his mind off the paralyzing cold.

The twilight deepened and the snow became heavier. Thomas realized that even if Coomy's friends at the gorge were lucky enough to spot the column, they probably would be able to do nothing more than fire a few shots. But he doubted that anyone on the rim of the gorge would be able to hear or see them in the snow, and with the wind howling the way it was. And the men were truly in no shape to attempt to kill the guards, and…

Thomas knew, as he had always known when it came time for him to act, that he could not now rely on Coomy's friends or on any of the other men in the column to make his escape, that he must do what must be done alone. If he failed, then he alone would die, but none of the men would die for — or because of — him.

He glanced over his shoulder. Hawkins was behind him, perhaps two or three paces back. His head was lowered; he probably hadn't looked up for hours, and wouldn't until the next head count was taken.

Thomas faced front again. There was nothing he could do any more for the men than he had already done, which had been considerably more than he had wanted to. He owed them nothing. He did not even share their belief in the cause for which they fought, and he surely didn't believe in their heaven or hell. All he had was his hate, and that was, for him, a stronger voice than their cause or their faith in God…

Even as these thoughts ran through Thomas' brain, he quickened his pace. A new-found strength surged through his body, and his heart began to race. He moved quickly, keeping his body in a low crouch. The pointed end of Jason's stick was in his right hand…

In a matter of moments he was to the right of, and slightly behind, the lieutenant. And then, because the wind came from that direction, he dropped back and quickly came to the other side, letting the blowing snow obscure him. For a short distance he moved parallel and in front of the rider. Then suddenly he turned and, with incredible swiftness, rushed at the lieutenant, making sure to stay behind the horse's line of sight.

In an instant, Thomas pulled the rider over to the left and low over the saddle bow with his left hand and simultaneously drove the pointed stick into the man's neck.

The lieutenant gave a soft moan and made some weak gurgling sounds. The horse sensed something was amiss, but Thomas grabbed hold of the bridle and quickly steadied him down. Holding the bridle with one hand and the dying lieutenant in the saddle with the other, Thomas quickened the animal's pace. When he was far enough in front of the column to risk a pause, he stopped and mounted behind the lieutenant.

Moments later he guided the animal south off the road, and once he gained the cover of the woods Thomas halted, turned and looked for the column. He could neither see it for the swirling snow, nor hear it because of the howling wind. When he was satisfied that it had passed, he continued to ride deeper into the woods.

After about an hour, Thomas stopped and let the lieutenant's body drop from the saddle. Then he dismounted and took the dead man's revolver, holster and ammunition.

Minutes later Thomas was in the saddle again.

FIVE

Late the following morning, Thomas came upon a small log cabin at the side of a frozen stream. He knew that if he didn't get some food and rest, he probably wouldn't last out the night. Not two hours before, he had fallen asleep in the saddle and almost blundered into a Union cavalry patrol. To allow himself to be recaptured would mean…

He dismissed the possibility from his mind and, dismounting, stood for a long time and watched the cabin.

The snow had stopped sometime earlier, and the wind had died down so that the gray smoke coming from the cabin's stone chimney went straight up and then spread out to look like a large turkey feather. There was a split rail fence around the cabin, but most of it was covered by snow. On the far side of the yard there was a shed, probably for a cow and a few pigs. The door to the cabin faced the stream.

Now and then Thomas caught the scent of bread being baked, and his empty stomach reacted with a violent fit of cramps. But it was the strong smell of coffee that made him mount up and gallop down to the front door. And he would have, if he had not caught sight of something moving in the woods on the other side of the stream.

Easing the carbine out of its sling, he dropped to his stomach and waited. In a matter of minutes five Union cavalrymen came down to the edge of the stream, crossed it and disappeared behind the front of the building.

Thomas sucked in his breath and slowly exhaled, blowing his steaming breath down toward the snow. He realized with some disgust that he was still behind the Union lines. Sometime during the night, he had obviously changed his direction. It had probably happened during the many times he had fallen asleep. He was annoyed with himself for having given into his weariness and for not knowing it sooner. The presence of so many Yankee cavalry units should have given him some idea that he had not crossed into Confederate territory.

He shook his head and, rubbing some snow over his face to wake himself up a bit more, he continued to watch the house. After not too much time had passed, the sound of a woman's laughter drifted up from the front of the cabin. This was followed by the more hearty laugh of several men. Then he heard nothing. But a few moments later he saw the first cavalryman slowly walk his mount over the frozen stream; another followed, and the third came next. By the time the fourth man came into view, Thomas became aware that there was something different about the men.

Then suddenly he realized that they were black. Taking it for granted that they were white like himself, Thomas had focused his attention on their uniforms and movements. But now that he had seen who they were, he began to wonder if they were out hunting him.

Thomas swallowed hard, and only when the fifth man crossed the frozen stream and disappeared into the woods did he relax his vigil. But he waited a good half-hour before he stood up and replaced the carbine in its sling. Then, glancing up at the cloud-covered sky, he decided to move back into the woods and wait until dark before going down to the farmhouse.

There was just the chance that the patrol would pass the same way on their way back to their unit later in the day or early evening. And rather than risk a shootout with them and probably getting himself killed or captured, Thomas was willing to endure the growling hunger, the numbing cold and paralyzing weariness for a few more hours.

But just as he was about to retreat into the woods, he saw a figure move out from behind the front of the cabin and walk slowly toward the shed on the other side of the yard. Whoever it was stopped and looked in his direction. But because of the trees and the distance, Thomas was sure he couldn't be seen.

He wondered if it was the woman whose laughter he had heard earlier. Or was it someone else? A husband, perhaps?

He shook his head. No matter who it was, if he offered any trouble when Thomas returned, he'd not hesitate to kill him, though that would not be the way he would want it.

Thomas eased his mount back a few paces and then, swinging into the saddle, he walked the horse deeper into the woods. But as he moved away from the cabin, he wondered about the people who lived there.

Suddenly Thomas found himself remembering the lovely mixed-race wench his middle brother Clem had bought in New Orleans. He tried to recall her name but couldn't. Clem believed in the South, in slavery, and in the right of a state to leave the Union. He believed and fought for these beliefs, and was killed for them at Vicksburg.

His brother John was against all that the South stood for, and he too fought for what he believed, only to be captured and sent to Libby Prison.

And as for himself, his reason for joining the Confederate Army had nothing to do with his feelings about the South and its cause. If anything, he detested slavery and he believed in a strong Union. His reason for fighting, now that he could look at it with a sense of detachment, was in a way pathetically stupid. Perhaps — if examined from a certain angle, the way a jeweler might rotate a diamond to look for flaws — even funny. For surely there must be some humor when a man runs from a hellish marriage straight into the greater hell of war. From the screaming of an unloved wife to the shriller screams of the wounded and the dying. From the bed of a mistress to the noise, confusion and danger of battle. And from the wrath of a father —

Abruptly Thomas stopped thinking and, in a passionate voice, addressed himself to the frozen landscape. 'Wait for me, Father,' he whispered, 'wait for me, old man … I'm coming home … wait for me, Father, so I can kill you. By the living God, Father, you owe me that much!'

A moment later he was bending low over the saddle and pulling up the collar of his coat to shield himself from the wind. Thomas hoped that by some miracle the day would pass faster than usual. But he knew there would be no such gift for him, that he would have to wait for the time to pass and as it started to snow again, he would have to suffer even more torments from the weather before he could turn back to the cabin.

It was well past twilight when Thomas returned to the clearing. Mercifully, the snow during the afternoon did not fall continuously but came in numerous fits and starts, none lasting more than a few minutes at the most. Even as he stood at the edge of the woods, looking at the yellowish light in the rear window of the cabin and smelling the strong odor of roasted beef, a sudden snow squall swirled out of the woods from the opposite side of the frozen stream. And like an enormous veil it dropped over the clearing and obscured it from Thomas' sight. But moments later, the wind-driven snow felt like needle pricks against his face and hands.

He couldn't wait any longer and, lowering his head deep into his upturned collar, he guided his mount around the edge of the clearing and toward the front of the cabin. Keeping close to the line of trees, he moved slowly. When he was just a few yards from the cabin, Thomas dismounted, unslung the carbine and listened very carefully for any sounds that might indicate the occupants of the cabin had become aware of his presence.

But the wailing of the wind was all he heard.

Thomas took a deep breath, patted the flanks of his horse and, swinging the carbine into a high port position, started to run for the door. The distance was no more than a dozen yards, but by the time he had traversed half of it, he was breathing hard and his body was soaked with perspiration.

He stumbled, but quickly regained his footing. Then the door was in front of him. Lifting his right foot, he drove it against the door, tearing the wooden hasp from its hinges and driving the door open.

He leaped inside and shouted, 'Everyone stand easy!'

The woman bent over the hearth stood erect and uttered a startled cry. The old man who was sitting in a rocking chair off to one side of the hearth, but close enough to it to feel the warmth of the fire, started to stand and cried, 'By Gward, a Confederate sojer!' And then he sat down again.

If they were surprised by Thomas' sudden entrance to their cabin, he was no less surprised to discover that both of them were black. The old man was kind of dark, with gray hair and a small gray beard. But the woman was much lighter, with very dark eyes and short, black, kinky hair.

'By Gward,' the old man said, 'he's a Confederate sojer fer real.'

'That's right, old man,' Thomas said sharply, 'I'm a Confederate officer.' And he kicked the door shut. Then he reached out and, drawing a rude chair to him, took a moment to wedge it against the door. When he was satisfied that a sudden gust of wind wouldn't blow the door open, he walked toward the fire and, looking at the woman, ordered her to put food on the table for him.

'Don't ya do it, Jenny,' the old man said. 'Don't ya set nothin' down fer no Confederate sojer.'

'Old man,' Thomas said, taking several steps deeper into the cabin, 'I don't want trouble, but if you give me any, it wouldn't bother me none to kill you.' And he swung the carbine in front of him to prove that he wasn't just making an idle threat. 'Now you tell me, what it's going to be?'

The old man snorted and, looking defiantly up at him, said, 'If'n Jenny's man wuz here, ya wouldn't be talkin' so stron'.'

The woman suddenly stepped between him and the old man. 'Pay no mind ta him,' she said. 'You sit down and I'll bring you victuals.'

For a few moments Thomas didn't move and neither did she. He found himself looking straight at her. She was a handsome woman, with features that suggested there was more than black and white blood in her. Probably Indian; at least, that was what her high cheekbones suggested. Though she wore a home-spun dress, it showed she had a well-developed body. And even as they stood there looking at each other, Thomas became very much aware of the agitated movement of her breasts under the rough cloth. The last time he had been close to a woman had been when he had gone to Richmond to see John. He shook his head to blot out the memory of that sad meeting. Then suddenly he realized he was pointing the muzzle of the carbine, and was touching her belly with it. He pulled it back and felt himself go hot with embarrassment.

'I'll sit at the table,' he said, taking a step back.

She shrugged and went back to the hearth to fetch a bowl of soup and bread.

Thomas went to the other side of the table. He sat down, placed the carbine across his knees, and, un-holstering his revolver, set it down on the table within easy reach of his right hand. For the first time since he entered the cabin, he looked around. Part of the room was curtained off and was, he guessed, where the woman slept. The old man's bunk was near the wall. The light he had seen coming through the window came from a coal oil lantern. The rest of the cabin was illuminated by two Betty lamps and the light from the fireplace.

The woman set the soup and bread in front of him.

'Much obliged,' he said with a nod, and immediately wolfed the bread down.

'You'd be more comfortable,' the woman suggested, standing close to the table and looking down at the tall, thin, bearded man, 'if you took your coat off.'

'Wot ya doin', woman,' the old man said, 'talkin' ta him like he wuz a friend? Don't ya know he's a reb?'

She didn't answer.

The old man mumbled something more about not wanting a 'Confederate sojer' in his house.

When Thomas was finished with the soup, the woman set a plate of beef in front of him and he attacked that with as much gusto as he had the soup and bread.

The woman sat down across from the man. She could see that his face and hands were raw from the cold, and even though his face was bearded, she could tell from the look in his eyes and the pull of his skin how tired he must be. She clasped her hands and rested them on the table. 'How long have you been out there?' she asked in a low voice.

Thomas swallowed a piece of meat before he said, 'I saw the cabin this morning, just before the blue-bellies came.'

She shook her head. 'I don't mean that,' she explained, 'I mean out in the snow —'

'Forever,' he answered. 'Two days and as many nights.'

Again she shook her head, but this time she did not speak.

'Ask him about his guns,' the old man said. 'I knowed fer a fact them's Yankee issue.'

'That's right, old man,' Thomas answered, sopping up the juice from the meat with a piece of bread. 'They belonged to a lieutenant.'

'You stole them.'

'No,' Thomas told him, 'I took them —'

'You stole them!'

'I took them after I killed him.'

The flat calmness of the man's voice made Jenny tremble. He spoke about killing the way other folk speak about the weather or some other little pieces of daily living.

Thomas saw the effect of his words on the woman and was sorry he had said them. And in an effort to make amends for frightening her, he complimented her cooking.

'No fancy words,' the old man told him. 'Ya had yer belly filled, now get goin'!'

Thomas stood up. The warmth of the room had finally taken the numbness out of his body. 'I can't ride anymore,' he said looking at the woman. 'My horse —'

'Not yer horse!' the old man exclaimed shrilly.

'Pa,' the woman said, 'please don't make no trouble.'

'He's a reb,' the old man said. 'A lousy no-good reb.'

'My horse,' Thomas said again, 'can't go on either. He needs food and rest.' Then he holstered his revolver and looked at the old man. 'She's going out with me, while I bed down my horse. If you make any kind of a fuss, I'll kill her. Do you understand?'

The old man's jaw went slack and his eyes became very wide.

Thomas tried to indicate to the woman that he didn't really mean what he had said, but hoped it would sufficiently frighten the old man to keep him from doing something that might get him killed. But if she understood the meaning of his raised eyebrows, she didn't let on.

'I'll be all right,' the woman said.

'Jenny,' the old man said, shaking his head, 'I won't do nothin'.'

'Better slip on your coat,' Thomas told her. 'It's bitter cold.'

The woman put on the same coat he had seen earlier in the day on the person in the yard. He guessed it had been her. But then he saw that there was only one coat and couldn't be sure who he had seen, though he knew that it made absolutely no difference.

'You first,' he said, gesturing with the carbine.

She went to the door and removed the chair. Moments later Thomas followed her out into the night and told her where he had left his mount. Then he said, 'I jest said that to your pa to make him behave.'

'He's frightened,' she said.

'I'm sorry, but —' He suddenly realized that he was about to apologize to her and stopped himself.

All the time that it took to bring the horse into the shed, unsaddle and feed him, neither of them spoke. But when they started back to the cabin, Thomas looked up at the sky. It was still cloudy, but was nowhere as thick as it had previously been. He guessed that the sky would be clear by morning, and said as much to the woman.

'Will you leave then?' she questioned.

'If I feel strong enough,' Thomas answered and then he asked where he was.

'Lukins' Farm,' she told him.

'I have to get back to my own lines,' he said.

The woman shook her head and, pointing first in one direction then to all the other points of the compass, she said, 'The Union troops are everywhere. You can't go south.'

'Which way can I go?' he asked, suddenly stopping and taking hold of her hand.

'West,' she told him, 'through the mountains.'

Thomas brought a picture of the map into his brain. On a straight line from where he had been captured, going west would take him to Missouri. He suddenly felt the woman trying to free her hand. Realizing he was holding it, he instantly released it.

SIX

Thomas slept in the rocking chair, which he had moved into a corner. From there he would have the advantage of not only being able to see the movements of the old man and the woman, but would have the drop on anyone who might enter the cabin.

The old man went to his bunk mumbling about how he wished the 'Union armies would git goin' and win da war.' But as soon as his head touched the corn husk mattress, he fell asleep.

The woman stayed up awhile longer. She sat on an old straight-backed wicker chair near the hearth and stared into the fire for a long time without speaking.

Her presence bothered Thomas, but he couldn't bring himself to tell her to go to bed. After all, it was her house and he certainly couldn't consider himself a guest.

Now and then he found himself staring at her. Once he tried to guess her age. She could have been a few years younger than himself, or a few years older. There was no way of knowing for certain which way it was.

'Where's your home?' the woman asked without looking at him, though for some time she felt his eyes on her.

He did not expect her to speak and did not feel obliged to answer.

She slowly turned her head toward him but did not repeat the question.

'Texas,' Thomas said. Her tan skin shimmered in the wavering firelight. 'From a ranch near a place called Paso Diablo.'

The woman nodded and, turning to stare into the fire again, said, 'Is that where you headin'?'

'Yes,' he answered.

Nothing more was said between them until she stood up and bade him goodnight. Thomas returned the courtesy and watched her as she walked across the room toward the curtain, then disappeared behind it. For a while he listened to her movements and was even able to tell when she laid down on her bed. But after that he couldn't keep his eyes open and, hoping that he would be able to hear anyone who approached, he drifted off to sleep.

Sometime during the night he dreamed about Lisa.

First he saw her lying on the bed naked waiting for him, and then he saw himself with her and felt the fragrant warmth of her body against his. It was a good dream, and it repeated itself over and over again in the many ways they had made love…

Suddenly Thomas was awake. His eyes went first to the old man: he was asleep. The curtain on the other side of the room was still closed. But from the gray light in the window he realized that it was almost dawn. Then suddenly, just as Thomas started to stand, he discovered an old army blanket had been thrown over him during the night.

His eyes went to the old man. He wouldn't have done it. He looked toward the curtain. That the woman could have come so close without waking him was surprising enough, but what he really found hard to understand was why she had made no attempt to overpower him? If she could place the blanket on him, she could have just as easily snatched the carbine, and that would have ended his chance to —

The curtain was suddenly pushed aside and the woman padded out. She was already dressed, except for her shoes, which she held in her left hand.

Thomas stood and held up the blanket. 'I'm much obliged,' he said.

The woman nodded and, setting her shoes down, began the work of building up the fire.

'Let me do that,' Thomas said, stepping forward.

She looked at him, then at his hands, one of which held the blanket and the other the carbine.

'All right,' Thomas said. He placed the blanket over the back of the rocking chair and set the carbine across the arm rests. Then he began the work of starting the fire going. But he was forced to stop several times. The task of carrying the large pieces of firewood was almost too much for him, and the wound in his shoulder seemed terribly sore. When he finally finished he was wet with sweat and so weak in the knees that he had to sit down on the rocking chair, or risk falling. The woman was looking at him.

'I'll be fine,' he tried to assure her, 'once I —'

'You're not fit to ride today,' she told him, 'and maybe not tomorrow either.'

Thomas shook his head.

'You leave,' she said in a matter-of-fact manner, 'you ain't never goin' to make it home. Either you'll be captured or die out there and become food for the wolves.'

Thomas took a deep breath. 'If I'm caught here,' he explained, 'you and your father —'

'My father-in-law,' she said correcting him.

'You'll be guilty of harboring a Confederate soldier.'

The woman lowered her eyes. 'Maybe the Lord understands,' she whispered, and then, looking straight at him, said, 'I don't want to go to my maker knowing I could have helped a man live but instead let him die.'

Thomas reached up, and with the tips of his fingers he gently touched her face. Though he wanted to thank her, he couldn't quite manage to get the words through the tight feeling in his throat.

When the old man awoke and the woman made breakfast for the three of them, she said, 'Pa, he's in no fit state to ride today.' She spoke without looking at her father-in-law or at the man she was talking about.

'But he's a Confederate sojer!' he exclaimed.

'Can't deny that,' she answered. 'But if he was wearin' the blue instead of the gray, would you help him?'

'That's a damn fool thing ta ask me, Jenny,' he said.

The woman nodded. 'I don't have any blue uniform for him,' she told her father-in-law, 'but I got some clothes around that might fit him.'

'They're Bob's?'

'He won't need them,' she said.

His old man looked as though he was about to say something more, but he just nodded and then busied himself with eating.

Later in the day the woman gave Thomas a pair of trousers, a shirt and a heavy sweater and told him to go behind the curtain to change.

'I want to look at your shoulder,' she called out.

'No need to bother,' he answered, slipping off his trousers. But to his surprise, she pushed the curtain aside and was there almost as he finished speaking.

'It's your shoulder I'm interested in,' she said. 'Now let me see it.'

Thomas undid the top buttons of his underwear and slipped it off. Even to him the wound looked raw and festering.

The woman examined it and said, 'This wasn't done by a bullet.'

'No,' he explained, 'I got in a fight with another prisoner. It was made by a pointed stick.'

She shook her head and made a low sound of disapproval. 'I'll boil up some water … needs washing, and a poultice wouldn't do it any harm.'

Thomas nodded, and later when she tended his wound he asked her about the Union patrol he had seen on the previous day.

'They stopped to say goodbye,' she explained as she placed a hot compress over the wound. 'They were leaving to go where the fighting is. The sergeant knew Bob —' She stopped, removed the compress and placed it in the boiling water. 'Did you ever fight against Negro troops?' she asked without looking at him.

'No,' he said, 'I never did.' He was sure that he heard her sigh with relief.

She came back to him with another compress. 'Bob was killed,' she said evenly as she pressed the steaming hot cloth against his shoulder.

'Does —'

'Pa knows,' she said, anticipating his question. 'But it makes him feel good to think that maybe, by some miracle, his son will come home when the war is over.'

'And don't you hope for a miracle too?' he asked, looking up at her. She was standing off to his side and bending over him. Her breasts were so close that if she took a deep breath they would have touched him.

'No,' she answered, moving away from him. 'And I hardly think you do either.'

Thomas chuckled. 'The closest I've ever come to one is this place here,' he said.

She shrugged but did not answer.

That night Thomas slept on the floor near the hearth. The woman had given him an old mattress and, with the blanket, he was considerably more comfortable than he had been in a long time.

By the end of the first week, he ventured to call the woman by her given name, Jenny, and the old man by his surname. But it took the better part of another week before she asked Thomas his name. Jenny always called him 'Mister Carey,' while her father-in-law preferred to address him as 'Lootenant Carey', though at the behest of Jenny, he promised never to mention Thomas' former military rank in front of strangers.

With food and rest, Thomas regained his strength quickly. His wound healed, leaving a scar no larger than a penny. And if it weren't for the weather, he might have left and tried to make his way west, to Missouri. He wasn't quite sure when he had made the decision to go that way instead of attempting to pass through the Northern lines and then go south. But the more he thought about Missouri the better he liked it. There was enough open space for a man to move around in, and too much of it for the Union cavalry to adequately patrol. From Missouri, he planned to slip across the border to Arkansas and then ride into Texas.

But for every day of sun, there were five of snow and as many days of terrible cold. Winter had started the night Thomas had stood in the doorway and watched the snow fall and cover the prison yard, and now, several weeks later, it had a frozen hold on the land and everything that lived on it.

Though neither Jenny nor her father-in-law would have dreamed of asking Thomas to help with the chores, such as going out to the shed to feed the livestock or doing some of the mending needed on the cabin and the shed, he took it on himself to perform these duties. He considered it small payment indeed for all that Jenny and Mr Lukins had given to him.

Before he realized it, according to the calendar that Jenny kept, it was almost Christmas time. And she commented that it would be nice if they had something special for dinner on Christmas Eve.

The following morning Thomas went out into the woods and quickly found deer tracks. By noon, he stalked and killed a young buck not three miles from the cabin. He slung the carcass over his shoulders and slowly made his way back to the cabin. But as he came into the clearing he spotted two riders coming across the frozen stream. He dropped the dead deer from his shoulders at the edge of the clearing and hoped that the wolves wouldn't get at it before he returned. Then he waited until both riders were behind the front of the cabin before he started to run across the clearing.

When Thomas reached the side of the cabin, he paused to catch his breath and set the carbine against the wall. From what he could hear both men were inside. His first thought was to enter and hope that his arrival would convince the men to act civilly toward Jenny and Mr Lukins.

Then suddenly Jenny screamed, the door opened and she came running out of the cabin with one of the men tailing right after her. The other man stood in the doorway, laughing. Thomas knew exactly what they intended to do to Jenny, but he still wanted to avoid a fight if it was at all possible.

'Ain't she a cute thin'!' the man chasing her said as he grabbed hold of her. 'Ah swear if she ain't as pretty a gal as I've ever had da pleasure of lookin' at.'

'Ya always say that,' the other man said. He stepped out of the doorway and slowly made his way to where his friend held Jenny.

Both of them wore the long gray coats supplied to Confederate soldiers, but underneath them, from what Thomas could see, they were dressed in civilian clothes. Then he noticed their boots: they were Western-style boots. Like himself, they were a long way from home — wherever it was. But he knew them for what they were; drifters. Men who would do anything to anyone for a price, or for their own pleasure. He had seen hundreds of men like them behind the Southern lines, or on a battlefield after the battle picking over the dead for what they could get.

'Ah can feel her heart just a-beatin' away,' the man said, clamping his hand over Jenny's breast. 'Gosh darn, she is sure a lot of woman. Ah toss ya who goes first.'

'Oh, God, no!' Jenny screamed as the taller of the two put his hand on her body.

'You're goin' enjoy it wid us,' he laughed, 'more than you ever had with your man.'

Thomas stepped around to the front of the house, hoping that the man who was holding Jenny would release her the moment he saw him. 'Gentlemen,' he said, 'you had best mount up and ride out.'

The man did release Jenny, and she ran off to one side.

The man with his back toward Thomas made a move to go after her.

'No!' Thomas said sharply.

The man stayed where he stood.

Suddenly the one facing him began to laugh. 'He don't have a gun,' he told his friend. 'Can ya beat that, he's standin' there tellin' us what ta do and he don't even have a gun in his hand. You go after the woman an' I'll take care of him.'

'Don't move!' Thomas said again.

The man with his back to Thomas said, 'Now this is downright foolishness, mister. She ain't worth dyin' fer.'

The one who spoke was the taller of the two. Something about him reminded Thomas of the man who had grabbed hold of his wife and had dragged her into the bedroom where he and his friend had raped her, while Zeb had held him at gunpoint in the living room. He still remembered how Helen had screamed! It had hardly seemed possible that such a small woman could have screamed so loud or so much.

Suddenly the man whipped around and started to go for his gun.

In an instant, Thomas drew and fired. The bullet smashed into the snow just in front of the man.

'The next one,' he said calmly, 'will kill you.'

The two of them looked at each other, and then the taller one licked his lips and said, 'We weren't lookin' fer any trouble, mister. We wuz jest driftin' west.'

'That's right,' the shorter one added, 'we didn't come here lookin' fer a woman neither.'

Thomas said nothing. His eyes narrowed down and he waited for one or both of them to move.

'We jest intended to stop an' rest fer a spell,' the short man said.

Thomas nodded. 'I could see that,' he answered, 'when I came around the side of the building … I could see exactly what you were doing.'

The tall man laughed nervously. 'There's no need fer ya ta get all riled up over that,' he said. 'We wuz jest havin' some fun. I mean, a wench like that thar jest sets a man a-goin'.'

'If we'd knowed ya had first call on her,' the smaller one explained, 'we'd-a never teched her.'

'We're powerful sorry 'bout that,' the other man said.

'I'm sure you are,' Thomas said. He paused, and then, in a monotone voice, added, 'That's just why I'm going to kill you. I don't want you to live too long and feel so powerful sorry.'

The shorter man began to move.

Thomas fired and blew apart the top of his head. He fell backward, splashing blood all over the snow.

Jenny gasped. The back of her hand flew to her mouth.

The tall man dropped to his knees and began to beg for his life.

Even as the smoke curled out of the barrel Thomas moved his hand slightly to the right and pulled the trigger. The bullet hit the man in the chest and knocked him over. Thomas walked to where the man lay and, standing over him, continued to fire. Each time a bullet struck the body it jumped.

When the revolver was finally empty, Thomas looked at Jenny and, in a flat voice, said, 'I'll bury them.' Then, glancing at the two horses, he added in the same emotionless voice, 'At least they had good mounts, even if they were buzzards.' He faced Jenny again. 'I brought down a deer,' he told her. 'It's at the edge of the clearing.' And he pointed to where it was. 'I'll bring it along later, after I —'

'Yes, yes,' she whispered.

'Mister Lukins?' he questioned.

'He was struck on the head,' she told him.

'Go tend him.'

Jenny nodded. As she passed Thomas, she stopped and, sobbing, flung herself into his arms.

'It's all right,' he told her, holding her close. 'It's all right now.'

SEVEN

That night the old man was too shaky to come to the table for dinner, and after Jenny fed him he fell asleep, leaving her and Thomas sitting in front of the hearth.

Thomas sat on the rocking chair, looking into the flames, but he was scarcely aware of them. He wasn't even thinking about the two men he had killed. But what had happened had brought back memories of the past that he had seldom allowed himself to think about, even when he had been in the army. Except for the time he had spent with Lisa, most of what he recalled was dark and filled with anger. He was still filled with anger, but the time was coming when he would go back and face up to his father. Perhaps, after he killed him —

'If it hadn't been for you,' Jenny suddenly said, 'they would have raped me.'

He turned and looked at her. She was sitting on the high-backed wicker chair.

'Yes,' he answered, and faced the hearth again.

'I've never seen a man kill another man,' she said after a long pause. There was more than a hint of fear in the tone of her voice.

'If I didn't do it,' he told her, 'they would have killed me.' He didn't want her to be afraid of him.

'Yes,' she said in a whisper, 'I know that. That's why I want to tell you that I'll never forget you, or what you did.'

'I've seen men just like them ruin a woman for life,' he said, still looking into the flames. 'Maybe that's why I wouldn't even give them a chance to draw.' He stood up and, bracing himself against the upper part of the hearth, said, 'I think I'd like to turn in now.'

She stood up and stepped behind him. 'Thank you,' she whispered, and gently placed her hand on his shoulder.

Thomas nodded and expected her to move away, but she didn't.

'I wish,' she said haltingly, 'that there was some way to repay you, but I have nothing to give —'

'You've already given me more than anyone I have ever known,' he said, turning toward her. 'You saved my life.'

'I did what any human being would have done for another. But what you did,' she told him, 'took courage. It's not every white man who'd risk his life to stop another white man from raping a Negro woman.'

'I don't think of what other men will do,' he said. 'I do what I think I should.'

'Yes,' she answered. 'I knew the first night you came here.' Then she turned and quickly went behind the curtain.

Sometime later when Thomas was already stretched out in front of the dying fire, Jenny called to him. He moved his head toward the curtain and saw her. 'What is it?' he asked, realizing that it was the first time he had ever seen her in a nightdress.

She didn't answer.

He rolled over on his stomach and, resting himself on his elbows, asked her what was wrong.

'I can't sleep,' Jenny told him. 'No, that's not it … I want you with me.' She stood looking down at him and after a few moments said, 'I wanted you to know.' And with that, she disappeared behind the curtain.

Thomas left his place in front of the hearth and went behind the curtain. Jenny was in bed, but he saw the nightdress lying over the back of a chair. He stripped off his long underwear and got into bed with her.

'Why?' he asked, placing his arm over her naked breasts and his hand on her shoulder.

'Because,' she answered, 'I've fallen in love with you.'

'You know I'm going to be moving on come spring?'

'Yes.'

Thomas touched her face and then kissed her. Slowly he caressed her warm supple body, moving over her naked breasts and down her flat belly until he reached her sex.

At the same time Jenny slipped her hands over his body, and when the time came for them to join, she moaned with delight.

Their lovemaking was so slow and passionate, and when they reached the throes of their passion Jenny called him by his given name over and over again, while he lost himself in the exquisite pleasure she so willingly gave.

Afterward they slept in each other's arms.

As the first gray light of day filled the window, Thomas awakened and kissed her gently on the lips. He started to leave, but Jenny touched his arm and said, 'There's no need to go.'

'Are you sure?' he asked.

'Yes,' she answered. 'I have been trying to think of some way to bring you to my bed,' she explained frankly, 'but nothing seemed right.'

'What about Mister Lukins?'

'He knows how I feel,' she said.

'You told him?' he asked, somewhat surprised.

She nodded.

Thomas didn't press Jenny for any more details. He took her into his arms and made love to her again.

The weeks that followed were, for Thomas, by far the most beautiful he had ever experienced with a woman. And yet he could not have said that he really loved Jenny, at least not in the way he remembered having loved Lisa. But there was a gentleness about Jenny that appealed to him, and he delighted in her deep and open desire to please him. Yet neither of them spoke of their past or discussed the future.

Though Thomas was physically contented, he was mentally restive. There was no way for him to stop thinking about his father or Helen. Sometimes he was sure that she had been responsible for what had happened between himself and his father. But he knew that wasn't true. If anything, Helen was as much a victim of the old man's will as he himself was...

One night after Thomas had made love to Jenny and they lay naked in each other's arms, she said, 'Somethin' more than just the war and its killin' is botherin' you ... somethin' that keeps pullin' on you to go back to Texas.'

'I've got a score to settle,' he answered.

'That means more killin',' she said.

'Sometimes,' he told her, 'that's the only way a man can have peace.'

Jenny remained silent for a long time. But then she said, 'It's you I'm worried about.'

He cupped her bare breast and nuzzled her neck. 'I know that,' he whispered. 'And I thank you for it.'

That was as close as Thomas ever got to telling Jenny that he was going home to kill his father.

Soon the days became noticeably longer, and though it still snowed from time to time, when the sun shone it was warm with the promise of spring. By the middle of March there was one whole week of warm sun-filled days. The snow began to melt in earnest and the ice on the stream beyond the fence thawed.

Then one day as Thomas was standing outside in the front yard watching the gray twilight shadows darken into evening, Jenny came out and stood alongside him. She took hold of his hand and, in a low voice, asked, 'When are you planning to go?'

Though he knew it would be soon, he hadn't really thought of a specific day. But since she had asked him, he thought it might be best to leave soon. 'The day after tomorrow,' he said, 'seems about as good as any other time.'

Jenny squeezed his hand, but she remained quiet.

'The longer I stay,' he told her, slipping his hand free of hers and placing his arm around her shoulders, 'the harder it's going to be when the time comes.'

'I know that,' she answered.

For several minutes neither one of them spoke. And in that time, the sky darkened and filled with the glint of stars.

'It has been good,' Thomas told her as he guided her back into the cabin.

'Yes,' she said. 'It has been very good.'

Thomas spent the following day getting his gear ready. And the next morning, though it looked as though it might rain before the afternoon, he left the Lukins' farm the same way he had come to it several months before, riding across the clearing to the rear of the cabin and then into the woods.

Sometime later he turned west, toward Missouri.

EIGHT

On a blistering afternoon in late June, Thomas reached the town of Pleasant Hill and decided to stop for a few hours' rest. He had been in the saddle since dawn, and the heat had sucked the strength out of him and his mount. Besides, a few hours one way or another wasn't going to mean anything to him or anyone else.

He dismounted and, leading his horse to the livery stable, told the boy there to feed and water the animal.

'That'll be a quarter,' the boy said.

Thomas dug down into his pocket. He didn't have more than a dollar, but nonetheless he fished out the required coin and tossed it at the boy, who caught it with one hand.

'I'll be around for him in a couple of hours,' he said and started up the street to the saloon.

A few minutes later, Thomas was seated in a cool corner drinking a beer. There were three men standing at the bar talking to each other and, except to be aware of their presence, he was too busy thinking about his own situation to pay any attention to them.

Ever since Thomas had entered Missouri, some two weeks earlier, he had been trying to find a place, first along the southern and more recently along the western border of the state, where he could have crossed into Arkansas or the Oklahoma Territory without having to run from or fight it out with a Union cavalry patrol. But as far as he could tell, it was almost as if the Yankees had placed giant doors on the borders and had swung them shut.

Thomas drained a bit more beer from the mug and hoped that he would have better luck where the Missouri and Nebraska borders touched. Then suddenly he realized that one of the three men at the bar had turned around and was looking at him.

He had done nothing to call attention to himself and he knew that he looked no different from any other drifter. His clothes were shabby and his chin unshaven. He probably stank from a combination of his own and his horse's sweat.

Thomas set the mug down and wondered whether he should leave before there was trouble. But as he thought about it, the other two men at the bar turned to face him, and he knew it was too late to do anything but wait for their next move.

He surely didn't want to become involved in a gunfight, especially with the odds against him, and with three men whom he had never seen before.

One of the men started toward him. He was tall and fair-skinned, with a shock of blond hair showing from under a wide-brimmed slouch hat. His eyes were light blue, but very bright, and his lids seemed heavier than those of other men. He was neatly dressed and, though he carried a forty-four, his hand made no movement toward it.

The other two men followed slightly behind him, one to the right and the other to the left. The man on the left was of medium height and carried himself like a soldier. The other was about the same height as the man in the middle, but he was less neatly dressed. Both of them were armed. Though neither one had his hand in position to draw, they looked as if they were fast.

Thomas started to stand, but the neatly dressed man motioned to him to remain seated. Then he said, 'I didn't mean to disturb you, stranger, but I always get curious when I see a man who looks like he has been riding for a spell.' His voice was pleasant, and there was a hint of a twinkle in his blue eyes and more than a suggestion of a smile at the corners of his thin lips. 'Mind if me and my friends join you?'

'No,' Thomas said. 'Go ahead and sit down.'

The man nodded to his companions and then the three of them sat down. 'Would you let me stand you a drink?' he asked.

Thomas nodded. 'That's mighty kind of you,' he said.

'I always follow the teaching of the Good Book,' he commented, 'which tells us more or less to do for others what you would have them do for yourself. Now, to me, you look like a man who would stand me a drink if our situations were reversed. Am I right?'

'I could hardly say you're wrong and still drink your beer,' Thomas answered with a thin smile. The man was obviously leading up to something.

'That's what I call an honest answer!' the man exclaimed, slapping the table and at the same time looking at his friends, who nodded their agreement, though their faces remained expressionless.

The man summoned the barkeep and ordered four beers. Then, looking at Thomas, he said, 'I also believe in Southern hospitality, and I can tell from the way you talk that you must too.'

'It's a fine tradition,' Thomas replied.

The barkeep hustled back to the table with the mugs of beer and set them down. The man shoved one toward Thomas, while his companions reached for theirs. He picked up the remaining mug and toasted, 'To the teachings of the Good Book and the fine tradition of Southern hospitality.'

Thomas nodded, reached across the table to touch the man's mug with his own, and repeated the gesture with each of the man's friends before he drank.

'Well,' the man said, 'there's nothing like friendly drinking to bring out the best in men.'

'Or the worst,' Thomas commented, setting his mug down.

The man smiled. 'Yes,' he agreed, 'I must admit that I have seen it go that way fairly often. But getting back to my reason for disturbing you,' he said, 'I was wondering what brings you this way?'

Thomas lifted his mug and took a long drink before he set it down and said, 'I'm going home.'

'And where might that be?'

'You *are* curious,' Thomas told him.

'Answer him,' snapped the man who carried himself like a soldier.

'Texas,' Thomas said, 'near the town of Paso Diablo.'

The neatly dressed man nodded. 'But you're heading in the wrong direction,' he commented.

Thomas took another drink of beer.

'Where are you coming from?' the man asked.

'East,' Thomas replied.

'How far east?'

'Virginia.'

The man with the military bearing sat back in his chair and said, 'I told you, he's nothing more than a lousy deserter.' And his hand went to his gun.

Thomas sensed what he was going to do, and without hesitating he drew. 'Now sit easy,' he told them, glancing at the men on either side of the table. 'One of you make a move and I'll blast your friend into the next world before either of you clears leather.'

No one moved, but the neatly dressed man said with obvious admiration, 'You're fast, mister, very fast.'

Thomas ignored the compliment and, looking at the man who had accused him of being a deserter, hotly told him his name, rank and the circumstances of his capture, leaving out the details of his encounter with Zeb. Then he said, 'Even if I wanted to get back to the Confederate lines, I couldn't get past the Yankee patrols.'

'I apologize for Captain Blunt's rash statement,' the man said. 'There are all too many Southern soldiers who have little or no sense of responsibility toward their country.'

'Which country is that?' Thomas questioned.

'The South, naturally,' he answered. 'Now, if you'll set your gun back in its holster,' he suggested, 'perhaps I might be of some assistance to you?'

'Why would you bother?'

'Because,' he answered with a smile, 'I have just returned from Richmond with others to raise an army to fight behind the Union lines. And that means the more experienced men I have, the better off I'll be.'

'Who are you?' Thomas asked.

'Colonel William Clarke Quantrill,' he said. 'I'm sure you have heard the name.'

Thomas nodded. 'A man can't ride from Kentucky to Missouri without hearing it,' he said.

Quantrill was obviously pleased by what he just heard, and smiled to show it. 'They're going to hear a lot more about me and my men,' he said.

Thomas made no comment. He didn't mention the fact that he had heard Quantrill's name long before he was captured, and that it was poor currency with his own troopers, who thought of Quantrill and his followers as nothing more than marauders and would not have hesitated to shoot them down on sight, if they had the chance.

'You already know Captain Blunt,' Quantrill said. 'My other companion is Dick Anders.'

Thomas flicked his eyes from Blunt to Anders. He could see that each of them was tensely waiting for the right moment to jump him.

'Now will you put your gun up and listen to my proposition?' Quantrill asked.

'I don't mean to seem unfriendly, colonel,' Thomas said, 'but for now I'd much rather keep things as they are.'

Quantrill's heavy lids closed until his eyes were narrowed down to mere slits. But still he managed an even voice and said, 'Ride with me and I'll make sure that you have decent clothes, a good mount and enough hard cash to make it worth your while. You can serve the South right here in Missouri. I'll give you your rank back.'

'You can't give me back,' Thomas told him, 'what no one has taken from me.'

'I'm afraid I didn't phrase that correctly,' he said. 'My apologies.'

'I accept them.'

'And my offer?' Quantrill asked. 'Do you accept that too?'

Thomas knew that if he rejected it, he probably wouldn't make it to the door before one or all three of them would open fire at him. 'Tempting,' he finally answered. 'Very tempting … but what made you approach me? After all, you couldn't have guessed —'

Quantrill started to laugh. 'Captain,' he said, 'would you like to tell him?'

'Your boots, lieutenant,' Blunt said. 'The colonel saw your Texas-style boots and noticed the way you wore your gun.'

'Details,' Quantrill said, cocking his head slightly toward Anders, 'often make the difference between life and death.'

Thomas saw the gesture, moved his right hand and pulled the trigger. The sound of the explosion filled the bar. Anders howled with pain and gripped his bloody right arm where the bullet had nicked it. The stench of burnt powder filled the corner of the room.

'Yes,' Thomas said calmly, 'details are very important.'

Quantrill's lids lowered again. Then he glanced at Anders and asked him if he was all right.

'Just a scratch,' Anders answered, glowering at Thomas.

Quantrill nodded and said, 'Are you going to throw in with me, lieutenant?'

'I don't see that I have much choice,' Thomas answered.

'By the living God,' Quantrill roared, 'I like that man.'

Thomas lowered his gun and slipped it back into the holster.

Quantrill ordered another round of beers and when the barkeep delivered them to the table, he toasted to a Confederate victory. And then he asked how Thomas thought the war was going.

'I wouldn't really know,' Thomas said. 'Sometimes we win, but even if we do, the Yankees always seem to come back for more.'

Quantrill nodded and said that he had been told by the Secretary of War that General Lee was going to move north again that very summer.

Thomas made no comment, and Quantrill didn't press him for one. He asked where Thomas' mount was.

'In the livery stable.'

'We might as well ride back to camp,' Quantrill said, and dropped a few silver coins on the table.

The four of them left the room together. Thomas walked with Quantrill, while Captain Blunt and Anders followed. When they were out on the street, Quantrill stopped and said, 'There's just one matter I want to clear up with you, lieutenant, before there's any further misunderstanding about it.'

'And what's that?' Thomas asked.

'Never draw on me again,' Quantrill told him, 'unless you intend to kill me.'

'I'll try to remember —'

Quantrill suddenly spun around and drove his fist into Thomas' stomach, doubling him up. A moment later he smashed his knee into the man's face; a torrent of blood poured from Thomas' nose.

'Anders, you have a score to settle with him,' Quantrill said. 'Do it now and let that be the end of it.'

Instantly Anders fell on Thomas, who was staggering back and forth, just managing to keep from falling. Again and again he punched him in the stomach.

'That's enough!' Quantrill ordered when Thomas began to vomit. 'Captain, get his mount from the livery stable and we'll ride back to camp.' Then looking at Thomas, who was hanging on to the hitching post for support, he said, 'I want you to keep a sharp eye on him … if he acts up, kill him. And that's an order.'

'Yes, sir,' Blunt answered with a salute.

'I don't think he'll give you any trouble,' Quantrill said with a smile. 'He's learned a hard lesson here this afternoon.'

For several days Thomas couldn't keep any food down, and was just able to stand muster each morning, then stagger back to the tent assigned to him by Quantrill. But even though he was in pain almost all of the time, he managed to get a good idea of the strength and kind of men who were part of Quantrill's raiders.

Of the sixty men in camp some were saddle bums, others were Confederate sympathizers. A few were obviously deserters from the Confederate Army, but most of the men were of a different ilk. They didn't much care on whose side they fought, as long as they had someone to fight and as long as there was the promise of good money, a plentiful supply of whiskey and little to stop them from looting and raping whenever and wherever possible.

Thomas also discovered that there was a Union counterpart to Quantrill's raiders, known as the Jayhawkers but also called Red Legs, because its men once wore red sheepskins for boot tops. And as he guessed, and was later told by one of the men in camp, there were hard feelings between the two groups, and many of Quantrill's raids in the past had been against the Jayhawkers.

On the morning of the fifth day, when the entire group of sixty-five men stood muster, Quantrill, mounted on a black stallion, asked Thomas to step forward. 'This man,' he announced to the assembled men, 'has been in camp for a few days. I know all of you have seen him and no doubt wondered who he is and what he is doing here. Unfortunately he met with some trouble and I could not introduce him to you until he recovered from the vicious beating he received from three Jayhawkers.'

A murmur of angry disapproval arose from the men.

'If it wasn't for our arrival,' Quantrill said, gesturing to Captain Blunt on his left and Anders on his right, 'the man would have been beaten to death. Anders there took a flesh wound to save him.' Then he smiled and said, 'Well, you can all see that he looks in good shape. Gentlemen, it gives me great pleasure to introduce Lieutenant Thomas Carey of the Confederate Army, who was captured in Virginia, managed to escape and having heard about us, came all the way out here to Missouri to join our army.'

The men cheered.

Quantrill held up his hand to quiet them. 'The lieutenant,' he said, 'will be given all the respect that goes with his rank. He will be in charge of the first troop. Now, just to show you how good he is — is there any man who would be willing to draw against him?'

Up until that moment Thomas was too astonished by Quantrill's performance not to feel a certain amount of admiration for the man. But now something else was happening and he didn't like it.

The men were talking among themselves.

'What?' Quantrill questioned. 'Not one taker?'

A few more moments passed and a short, lean man with fiery red hair stepped forward. 'I'll throw down wid him,' the man said.

The men fell silent, but there was a sudden tenseness in the air, the way it sometimes feels before a summer thunderstorm.

Quantrill laughed and said, 'Why is it always the little man who itches to cut down the big man?'

'Makes no difference how tall da bastard iz,' the red-headed man said with a deadpan face, 'this will bring him down ta size.' And he patted his holster.

'All right, Lem,' Quantrill told him, 'I sort of guessed you wouldn't be able to resist.' He looked down at Thomas. 'One draw and one shot,' he said.

'I have no reason —'

'If you don't,' Quantrill said, 'your life won't be worth much around here.' He looked toward Lem. 'One draw and one shot

… but for God's sakes, Lem, shoot in front of him. I have no use for a dead lieutenant.'

'I'm a'ready fer him,' Lem announced.

Thomas suddenly understood what Quantrill was doing, and he looked up and nodded.

'Whenever you gentlemen are ready,' Quantrill said.

Thomas moved away from the colonel's mount and glanced at the men. There wasn't a pair of eyes amongst them that did not gleam with pleasure. They reminded him of a pack of wolves waiting for one of their pack to make the kill before they moved in to tear it to pieces.

He flicked his eyes back toward Lem and started walking toward him.

Lem stood very still.

Thomas continued to move in close.

'He's goin' to trample him before he draws,' one of the men said.

The man laughed nervously.

But even as the laughter hung on the hot morning air, Thomas drew and fired.

Lem's hand had just pulled his revolver clear of the holster when the sharp single report exploded. The bullet slammed into the brown dry earth in front of him, causing a sudden eruption of bits and pieces of it.

'Damn if'n I saw his hand move!' one of the men exclaimed.

'Me neither!' another said.

'That was good shooting, lieutenant,' Quantrill called out.

Thomas glanced back at him and nodded. Then he looked at Lem. From the expression on the man's face, he guessed that he had probably made an enemy out of him. And that was something he could ill afford to do, especially since he knew that Captain Blunt and Anders already had hard feelings for him.

A few moments later Quantrill told the group that they would soon be riding against 'another nest of Jayhawkers', and then Captain Blunt dismissed them.

As soon as the men broke from the ragged formation, they swarmed around Thomas and congratulated him for what they had just seen him do.

NINE

Having proved himself to the men in the only way that really mattered to them, Thomas found that many of them were eager to become friends of his. Though he was always courteous, he did not form any close association and quickly gained a reputation for being a loner.

As for Thomas' rank, it hardly mattered, since little or no actual military discipline was followed. But it did mean that he rode at the side of Captain Blunt, who was always watching him.

Another week passed without anything happening, and during this time Thomas learned about Special Order No. 47, which had been issued by the Union General James Totten sometime in 1862 and declared Quantrill and all of his men outlaws. He also realized that most of the raiders were dead shots with revolvers, few were armed with carbines, and some had the old Sharps rifles.

Then, late one Friday afternoon, Quantrill assembled the men and told them that they were going to pay a visit to the three Jayhawkers who beat 'Lieutenant Thomas Carey.' The men responded with a loud cheer, and in a few minutes they were mounted and ready to ride.

To Thomas' surprise, Quantrill headed the column east and then swung south.

'Can you guess where we're going?' Captain Blunt asked.

Thomas shook his head.

Blunt smiled. 'I guess you weren't in any condition to take notice of the way we took you out of Pleasant Hill.'

'All I remember,' Thomas answered, 'was the roaring pain in my head.'

Blunt nodded and said nothing more.

The column continued to move without pausing to rest until the twilight had given way to darkness. But then Quantrill ordered a halt and, summoning the captain and Thomas, told them that their objective was a farm about three miles from where they were. He divided the group into five parts. Four would attack the farmhouse, kill every male found, and then fire the house and barn. Thomas was ordered to hold the fifth group of twelve men on a ridge in the event that the attackers might run into unforeseen trouble and find themselves under attack from some other Jayhawkers. 'But I don't think that will happen,' Quantrill said.

'Whose farm is it?' Thomas asked.

'Why, the man who beat you up,' Quantrill laughed. 'He lives there with his two brothers, his wife and his daughter.'

'Maybe,' Anders said, who always stayed close to Quantrill, 'the lieutenant don't have no guts fer this kinda thing. But don't worry none, lieutenant, you won't be close enough to get kilt.'

'You're pushing, Anders,' Thomas said. 'You're pushing and I don't like it.'

'Is that a fact?'

'Anders,' Quantrill said sharply, 'you evened your score outside of the saloon. Now I'm ordering you to stop riling him. And as for you, lieutenant, I wouldn't be so fast to take offense if I were you. Anders is a good deal better on the draw than Lem was.'

'Someday,' Thomas said, 'I'll just have to see how good he really is.'

'That will be enough of that, lieutenant!' Quantrill ordered.

'Yes, sir, colonel,' Thomas answered, but there was sufficient mockery in the tone of his voice to make Quantrill glare at him through his lowered eyelids.

The attack on the farmhouse took place shortly before midnight. A single shot fired by Quantrill brought the four groups of men galloping toward the house.

From the ridge where Thomas was stationed he saw the flashes of red flame from the guns of the marauders as they swept down on the farmhouse. The sounds of broken glass mingled with the staccato firing and the shouting of the men.

The raiders circled the farmhouse and galloped around it Indian fashion, pouring fire into every window. Then suddenly the barn door opened and several men ran forward and began to fire at the raiders, dropping three. But in a matter of moments they were cut down.

The shooting stopped abruptly.

Thomas could see the riders gathering in front of the house. Several of them dismounted and went inside.

After the tumult of shooting and shouting the night seemed even quieter than it had been before the attack. But then the silence was slashed by the shrill screams of the women, immediately followed by several angry shouts from the men.

'Gawd,' one of the men with Thomas exclaimed, 'I sure wish they'd leave sompin' fer us.'

'Don't think de womens'll be much good fer using when we gets there,' another man said.

The screaming continued for a long time, and then it stopped.

Soon a rider came toward the ridge and, when he was within hailing distance, shouted up that Quantrill wanted the lieutenant and his men to join the main force. Then he turned and raced back to the farmhouse.

Thomas at the head of his twelve men galloped down from the ridge and started to go toward Quantrill, while his men rode to where the other raiders were gathered.

Thomas slowed his mount and edged it close to the edge of the torch-lit group.

The men had formed something of a circle around the mother and the daughter. Both women were naked and spread-eagled. Now and then a man would step out of the circle and rape one or the other. Neither of the women looked as if they knew what was happening to them. In the torchlight their eyes were wide and staring, and a great deal of spittle ran from the mother's mouth. And every once in a while the daughter passed out, but she was immediately revived by having a pail of water thrown in her face.

Thomas took a deep breath. In all his years of fighting he had never seen anything like that. He turned his mount away and rode toward Quantrill. 'Those women won't last much longer,' he said.

Quantrill shrugged. 'I'm not brave enough to stop them,' he said. And then he asked, 'Are you?'

Thomas shook his head.

'Then in that case,' Quantrill told him, 'get some of those men who have already had their fun to start burning this place.'

Before half the men had used them the daughter died. The mother would have been raped by the others if it had not been for the fact that Quantrill was afraid that the light from the fire would be seen by other Jayhawkers in the vicinity. He ordered the men to mount and though they obeyed, it was not without much angry grumbling.

It was not yet twelve-thirty when the marauders began their march. Thomas looked behind him. The light from the fire cast a red glow in the night sky. He glanced up and saw that a cloud cover was beginning to form. Part of it had already settled over the burning house, which accounted for the red glow.

He tapped Blunt's arm and pointed up to the clouds and back toward the fire.

'Let's hope it starts to rain,' the captain said, 'before anyone becomes curious about that red glow.'

A few minutes later the first drops of rain fell, and then it came down in torrents. Quantrill quickened the column's pace, but the ground became too soft to go at anything more than a walk.

'I don't think we'll be able to make it back tonight,' Quantrill called back to Blunt. 'But I know of an abandoned farmhouse where we can stop until the morning.'

'That's all right with me,' Blunt answered, 'as long as we get out of this damn rain.'

Thomas would have preferred to put as much distance as possible between the column and the burning house, especially since they were leaving a trail in the soft wet earth. But rather than risk an argument with Quantrill or Anders, he decided to keep his opinion to himself. He hoped that Quantrill would only tarry at the farmhouse as long as the rain continued and that once it stopped he would move the column back to the camp site.

After about an hour they reached the farmhouse. It wasn't really large enough to hold all of the men, but they made do with the space available. The three wounded men were placed against the wall, near the hearth, but Quantrill would not allow a fire to be made. Shortly after they were set down on the floor, one of the men rolled over to one side and died. He had taken a stomach wound and there was small chance that he would have lived under any circumstances. One of the other men had had his left knee blown away, and the other had taken a bullet in his right shoulder. Both men groaned a good deal, but no one paid any attention to them.

A three-man guard detail was sent down the road as soon as they arrived at the farmhouse, and at two-hour intervals was relieved by another group of three men. Toward morning the rain stopped and the sun came, turning the heavy mist a grayish yellow.

The guard detail was called back and Thomas expected Quantrill to order the men to mount up and move out, but instead he told them that it might be worthwhile to spend the rest of the day there and return to their own camp that night. 'In the meantime,' he suggested, 'you men might dry out your blankets and other gear by hanging them on the fence.'

'If we're going to stay here,' Thomas said, going up to Quantrill, 'I think you should put out some pickets.'

Lem was close by and he had heard what Thomas had said. 'If'n somebody wuz lookin' fer us,' he commented, 'they'd have been here 'fore now. Ya not gettin' jumpy, are ya, lootenant?'

'I think Lem's right,' Anders said.

'What about you, captain?' Quantrill asked. 'Do you think we should put out pickets?'

To Thomas' surprise, Blunt nodded and said, 'Sometimes, colonel, an ounce of prevention is worth a pound of cure.'

'All right, lieutenant,' Quantrill said, 'take as many men as you need and put them where you want them.'

Thomas nodded, chose four men and placed them around the farmhouse.

As soon as Thomas returned, Lem came up to him and said in a loud voice, 'I ain't going ta be one of your picket boys … I want ya ta know that, so ya don't bother me none when I'm a-sleepin'.'

'Don't pick a fight now, Lem,' Anders said with a laugh, 'the lieutenant is plum worried about his pickets.'

Thomas flicked his eyes over to Anders and then back to Lem. 'If I need you,' he said in a low voice, 'I'll wake you.' And he started to turn away.

Lem grabbed hold of his arm and stopped Thomas. 'I already tol' ya not ta bother me,' he said. 'An' I meant it.'

'He's bigger than you are, Lem,' Anders said. 'I wouldn't mess none with a real live lieutenant.'

'I'm about ready ta cut him down to size,' Lem said.

'Go to it!' Anders exclaimed.

Lem went for his gun, but Thomas already had his clear of the holster and fired. There was a sharp explosion and Lem looked as if he had suddenly jumped. Then he fell backward.

Even as the smoke curled out of the end of the Colt's long barrel, Thomas pulled back his hand and pushed the revolver back into its holster.

A man bent over Lem and, looking at Quantrill, said, 'He's dead.'

'I didn't think he would have been anything else,' the colonel said. 'A couple of you men bury him and the other man in the yard.'

Thomas looked at Anders and said, 'If I ever find you setting another man against me, I'll kill you.' He faced Quantrill. 'Tell him that, colonel, if you want him to stay alive.' Then he walked out of the farmhouse, across the mist-enshrouded front yard, and leaned on the fence.

The mist on the distant hill was beginning to lift, and as Thomas watched it, he realized that he was doing what Mr Coomy had dreamed of doing, and what he himself had not wanted to do then or now. As far as he was concerned, he was finished with the war the moment he had met up with Zeb. And at night he still dreamed about going home to kill his father. That, and only that, was his war.

This business of riding with Quantrill against the Jayhawkers, or even against Union troops, was not to his liking. As Anders rightly had said, he had no stomach for it. To throw down with a man like Lem was one thing, but to be part of a gang of marauders who raped and burned made Thomas feel less of a man than he knew himself to be.

He took a deep breath and sucked in the clean morning air. Then he slowly exhaled. There was practically no chance in the foreseeable future for him to leave Quantrill and continue his journey home. For one thing the borders were closed, and for another —

Suddenly there was the sound of footsteps behind him. His hand dropped to his holster and as he drew, he spun around.

'You're on edge,' Captain Blunt said, holding his hands up to indicate that he had not come looking for a fight.

Thomas holstered his revolver.

The captain lowered his hands and came up to the fence. 'Most of the men,' he said, 'feel it was a fair fight. Lem would have killed you —'

'It's hardly worth talking about,' Thomas said.

'I guess not,' Blunt answered.

For several moments neither man spoke, then Blunt commented, 'Anders is mean … I wouldn't turn my back on him, as the expression goes, if I were you.'

Thomas nodded.

'And he has many friends in this group and in the others.'

'What others?' Thomas asked.

Blunt looked at him. 'Don't tell me you think that these men are all that Quantrill — I mean the colonel has following him?'

'I wondered about it,' Thomas admitted, 'but I figured I'd find out sooner or later.'

'There are a half-dozen camps like ours in various parts of Jackson, Clay and Cass counties.'

'Why are you telling me this?' Thomas asked. The morning stillness was suddenly ruptured by the sound of shooting, and then, from the hill directly in front of them where Thomas had stationed a picket, came the warning shouts that Union cavalry was approaching.

Thomas and Blunt ran for the house.

Quantrill came to the door. 'What's going on?' he called.

'Troops are coming up the other side of the hill,' Blunt shouted.

Several more shots sounded out.

Quantrill swore, and even as Blunt and Thomas rushed into the door of the farmhouse the first line of Union cavalry breasted the hill and was slowly moving down it. Another line came to the top and started down the long slope, and another line…

When the last line came into view Thomas counted two hundred and sixty-five men. But they stopped.

'We'll be able to hold them off,' Quantrill said, looking out of the door.

'Not for very long,' Blunt commented.

'They have four times our number,' Thomas said. 'And they have carbines … they don't have to come in close.'

Blunt agreed.

'If we can't hold them off and we can't run,' Quantrill questioned, 'what the hell can we do?'

'Get the horses saddled,' he said, 'and hold them out back in the ravine. Then put as many men as possible behind the hedges of the horse lot.'

'Anders,' barked Quantrill, 'get the men up to the bushes. Dooly, see that the horses are saddled and ready to move.'

One by one the men moved out of the farmhouse in a running crouch. Most of them took up positions behind the hedges, while some went out the back window to saddle the mounts.

Thomas and Blunt went to the hedges. The sun had burned off all of the mist. It was bright yellow and very hot.

'They must have followed us all night,' Blunt said in a throaty whisper.

'We sure made it easy for them,' Thomas said, 'with the kind of trail we left.'

'What are they waiting for?' Quantrill asked.

'Colonel,' Thomas answered, 'they have all the time in the world. Be thankful that they stopped long enough to let us get into position.'

Several minutes passed and nothing happened, but then Thomas saw the men in the first rank unsling their carbines. 'They're coming!' he exclaimed as the first line of sixty men began moving at a walk. 'They're going to make a frontal assault. Pass the word that no man fires until they wheel to the right.'

'How do you know they won't go left?' Quantrill asked.

'The space between the house and the barn is too narrow for them —'

'Anders,' Quantrill said, 'no one fires until the lieutenant does.'

'They're moving faster!' Blunt exclaimed. Thomas caught the quavering note in his voice. He looked at him.

The captain's face was a pasty white. The man was frightened.

'This is the first time I have ever faced Union regulars,' Blunt whispered.

'They die just as easily and as hard as Jayhawkers,' Thomas said, and turned his attention to the line of blue-uniformed men who were now shouting as they galloped toward them. At this moment his own heart began to race. He could hear the blood roaring through his head. The pounding hooves made the ground tremble.

Thomas glanced up at the sun and guessed that it was probably no more than nine o'clock in the morning. He wiped the sweat from his brow, and just as the sixty troopers thundered into the front yard, he slowly raised his revolver.

The cavalry men opened fire, sending three quick fusillades into the door and windows, before they started to wheel to the right.

'Steady!' Thomas whispered. 'Steady!' He glanced at the men. They held their revolvers ready.

The first men galloped in front of them.

Thomas sighted a man and followed him for a few moments. Then he fired. The trooper pitched from his mount.

Instantly a ragged volley belched out from behind the bushes. Several of the troopers were hit. Others tried to swing around in saddles and return the fire.

Thomas continued to pull the trigger until the cylinder was empty. The sharp stench of burnt powder filled the air.

The troopers swung back up the hill.

'Get those carbines,' Thomas shouted, dashing forward to the dead blue-belly nearest to him. Moments later, he was back with a carbine and the ammunition for it. Several raiders followed his example until the fifteen dead cavalry men were stripped of their arms.

'They're dismounting,' Anders said, standing up. An instant later a volley fire exploded from the Union troops. Anders was dead before he dropped to the ground.

'You men with carbines,' Thomas shouted, 'fire back at them.'

'We'll be cut to ribbons,' Blunt said hoarsely, 'if we stay here.'

Quantrill looked questioningly at Thomas.

'Our only hope is to get to the ravine,' Thomas told him. 'There's enough cover there to give us some chance.'

'But how are we going to get there?'

'The men with carbines and rifles will cover the rest of us,' Thomas told him. 'Those men who fall back will crawl until they reach the side of the house.'

Quantrill passed the order. Almost immediately the men began to drop to the ground and began to belly their way across the open space to the safety of the house.

'I'll stay,' Thomas said, 'and make sure that those with carbines continue to fire.'

Quantrill nodded and began to worm his way to safety.

'Take care,' Blunt said, and followed the colonel.

One of the men firing a carbine screamed and dropped back.

Thomas moved in a crouch toward him. The man was shot through the throat. Thomas picked up the carbine and began firing until it was empty. It was hard to see if any of the troopers on the hill had been hit, but two more men behind the hedges went down.

'All right,' Thomas told those who were left, 'fall back to the ravine.'

As soon as they stopped firing, the Union troops began to advance.

The distance between the hedges and the side of the house was not more than fifty yards, but it seemed like five times that as Thomas crouched and ran, dropped to his stomach and crawled, then crouched and ran again.

The troopers continued to fire until they gained the front yard, but by that time Thomas and the rest of the men had reached the heavy bushes along the rim of the ravine.

'Lieutenant?' Quantrill called just as Thomas rolled behind a thick bush. 'Over here.'

Thomas took a deep breath and quickly scurried to where Quantrill was. 'Where's Captain Blunt?' Thomas asked.

Quantrill pointed to a form lying under a nearby bush. 'He took one in the back,' he said. 'He must have stood up too soon … but he managed to crawl here.'

'Dead?' Thomas questioned, as he quickly reloaded his Colt.

'Near to it,' Quantrill answered.

Suddenly the Union troops ran out from behind the side of the house. And as they came, they fired.

Quantrill's men returned the fire. Several troopers dropped screaming in agony. But they continued to come, and Thomas knew that it was going to be a matter of every man for himself.

In moments the troopers were down in the ravine. And already some of the raiders were fighting hand-to-hand with the troopers.

Thomas and Quantrill drew back to where the growth was heavier. Men were shouting all around them.

'Which way are the horses?' Thomas asked.

'Up that way,' Quantrill said, pointing toward the west.

At that instant a trooper came at Thomas, swinging his carbine as though it were a club. Thomas dropped low and pushed the muzzle on his own weapon into the man's stomach. He pulled the trigger. The man screamed and fell backward.

The heavy growth made it impossible for raider and trooper alike to see whether a man was a friend or foe. But the animal instincts of each man guided him to his opposite. The hand-to-hand fight was desperate. The air was filled with shouts and curses, with screams and moans. So close was the fighting that only sporadic firing took place.

Thomas began to work his way toward the horses. But the troopers pressed the raiders with such ferocity that they were forced up one side of the ravine, and the instant they broke from the cover of the heavy growth, a burst of fire from the rim killed a number of them and compelled the rest to scramble back into the thick bushes.

Thomas spotted Quantrill and went toward him. Suddenly out of the corner of his left eye he caught the gleam of a saber. He squeezed the trigger of his Colt. A man screamed, and the next instant Thomas felt the searing bite of the saber on his left arm. But the trooper dropped in front of him. His face had been blown away and only the initial momentum of his thrust had carried the blade to its mark.

Thomas leaped over the dead man and joined up with Quantrill. 'Listen,' he said breathless, as he tried to stanch the blood pouring out of his wound, 'if we rush them, we might make for the other part of this ravine.' He didn't wait to hear whether Quantrill agreed with him. 'Pass the word that we'll charge when they hear me yell.'

Quantrill slipped away, and after a few minutes he came back. 'It's done,' he said.

'All right,' Thomas said, 'now.' And leaping to his feet, he shouted, 'Charge!'

The raiders picked up his cry and with blazing guns drove through the troopers' ranks, killing so many in the initial withering blast of fire that the others fell back, leaving the way open for Thomas and Quantrill to lead the men to another branch of the ravine. By the time they scrambled down the steep slopes to the safety of several thick hedges, there were not many raiders left and Quantrill took a bullet in the thigh. The troopers followed, but the slopes of the ravine were steep, and once they started down they were easy targets for the raiders.

The battle continued for more than an hour and a half, and then the cavalry men made one last charge and were driven back, taking heavy losses. Exhausted and almost out of ammunition, the raiders lay at the bottom of the ravine for the better part of two hours before Quantrill ordered two of the men to the edge to see what was happening.

Thomas looked around. Of the sixty-five men that had left camp the previous night, only twenty-one were left, and a good many of these were wounded.

'The blue-bellies done cleared out!' one of the men called from the edge of the ravine.

Thomas scurried up to the top. It was true. Whoever commanded the troopers had had enough. There were carbines and side arms all over the ground, and the pungent odor of burnt powder still hung in the air. But it was much cooler than it was in the sun-scorched ravine. He wiped his sweaty face with his neckerchief, then, sliding down the steep side, said to Quantrill, 'I guess we can move out.'

'Better see if we have any mounts left,' Quantrill told him. He pointed to Thomas' wound. 'That didn't stop you much from handling a gun,' he laughed drily.

'About as much as that stopped you from running,' Thomas said, pointing to Quantrill's wounded thigh.

Both men laughed, and then Thomas went for the horses. He found them where Quantrill said they would be, and swinging into the saddle he started to work the mounts toward the ravine.

Sometime later when the raiders were moving slowly across country, Quantrill turned to Thomas and said, 'I'll get the credit for this, but if it wasn't for you, I wouldn't be around to tell everybody how I managed to outfight several squadrons of Union cavalry.'

'I didn't doubt,' Thomas said, 'that you would have told it any other way.'

Quantrill laughed. 'You know,' he said, 'I think you're beginning to understand me.'

Thomas shook his head. 'I don't even try, colonel,' he replied. 'It's not worth my time or effort.'

TEN

Quantrill's stand near Pleasant Hill won him praise from the Confederate sympathizers in the three counties of Jackson, Cass and Clay that lay along the western border of Missouri. And of course, it also gained him plaudits from the rest of his followers. But it quickly got to the point where Quantrill himself began to believe that he and he alone was responsible for what happened that day.

At first Thomas found this somewhat humorous, though later he began to sense that there was something else behind Quantrill's play-acting, something that was more meaningful than his need to be a hero.

Because Thomas was with Quantrill at Pleasant Hill, he had earned a certain place in the ranks of Quantrill's raiders, as had all the other men who had managed to survive that bloody encounter. But Thomas' status among the men was enhanced because Quantrill kept him almost constantly at his side. Thomas not only took Anders' place, but since Captain Blunt had also been killed at Pleasant Hill, Thomas also became Quantrill's military advisor.

The shootout between Thomas and Lem in the farmhouse was never mentioned by any of the men who had witnessed it. He never knew, and really wasn't interested, whether Quantrill had something to do with the absolute lack of comment about it or not, since he believed — as Blunt had told him — that almost everyone who had seen it had said it was a fair fight.

June quickly passed ,and on July first word came to Quantrill in the late afternoon that General Lee had marched into

Pennsylvania and had met the Union army at a place called Gettysburg. Quantrill was elated and gathering the men together in the camp where he was at the time, he told them that the South would surely win a great victory. Then he turned to Thomas and said, 'The lieutenant will tell you that I'm not wrong, men. Go ahead, tell them how Lee is going to beat the Union army and then march on to Washington.'

Thomas was silent for several moments. He looked around at the men in the field. There must have been a hundred pairs of eyes staring up at him. Some of them were Confederate Regulars who had been sent to Quantrill by the Confederate Army to build up his force, but the others were all raiders.

'Well, speak up, lieutenant!' Quantrill urged.

'He might do it,' Thomas said, 'if he's lucky.'

A look of surprise passed over Quantrill's face, but he quickly regained his composure and he laughed. 'Leave it to a military man to play his cards close to his vest. What the lieutenant means,' he went on, 'is that Lee has the best damn army this world has ever seen, and since he is the best damn general, he will do it. Believe me men, when I tell you that Lee's men will be in Washington in just a few days.'

Later when they were alone in Quantrill's tent, he commented sharply, 'If you had backed me up at Pleasant Hill the way you did in front of the men, neither of us would be here now.'

'You asked me,' Thomas replied, 'and I told you.' He wasn't going to offer any apology for not sounding off the way Quantrill would have wanted him to. Playing soldier the way Quantrill did had little or nothing to do with fighting a real battle. Quantrill might be able to pull the horse's tail, so to speak, but that was a far cry from a battle between two trained armies.

'I swear,' Quantrill exclaimed, 'I can't figure you out. You fought for the South … you were a regular demon at Pleasant Hill, but sometimes I get the feeling that you don't really care if the Confederacy wins or loses.'

Thomas shrugged but did not answer.

By the fifth of June, the battle at Gettysburg was all over. It had ended the day before when Lee had thrown his forces at the Union army and had been hurled back with heavy losses. The Army of Northern Virginia was in full retreat.

This turn of events drove Quantrill into a wild frenzy. In a matter of days his raiders struck the farms of several Jayhawkers and ambushed a patrol of Union cavalry. He railed against the incompetence of Lee and his staff and swore that he would win the kind of victory that would give the people of the South something to be proud of.

'If we could do it at Pleasant Hill,' Quantrill told his men, 'with enough men, we could do it anyplace!'

By anyplace, Thomas soon discovered, Quantrill meant the city of Lawrence, Kansas, which in his opinion was the center of all Jayhawk activity along the Missouri-Kansas border.

Whenever Quantrill addressed the men, he never missed the chance to bring up his victory at Pleasant Hill and tell them that an even bigger one would be theirs if they took Lawrence. And it wasn't long before the raiders began to believe him. Even those who were not at Pleasant Hill were made to feel that they had taken part in the action.

Then, toward the latter part of July, Quantrill called all his leaders together. They met in a farmhouse of a known Confederate sympathizer. These were men whom Thomas had come to know as he had traveled with Quantrill from camp to camp.

Bloody Bill Anderson arrived at sundown. He was followed by George Todd, who had let it be known more than once that if anything ever happened to Quantrill, he would become the leader of the raiders. Bill Gregg, Cole Younger, Dick Maddox, and George Shepard came with their bodyguards.

The heat of the day lingered without the hint of a breeze to bring the promise of relief. Quantrill sat behind a table that was set up in the living room. His face glistened with sweat. Thomas stood off to one side, while the leaders sat wherever they could find a place for themselves in front of Quantrill.

Before the meeting started, a jug of corn whiskey was passed around, and after everyone in the room took a hearty swig, Quantrill rapped the barrel of his revolver on the table for silence. The men quickly became quiet.

Quantrill stood up and said, 'I brought all of you here because what I have to tell you is important and, as you will see, needs the cooperation of everyone in this room.'

'Jest tell us straight wot's on yer mind,' George Todd said, 'and cut all the fancy talk.' And he bit off another wad of chewing tobacco.

'Let him talk,' Younger commented. 'You ain't about to change his ways.'

Some of the other men laughed.

'All of you,' Quantrill said, 'know what's happening in the east.'

'That's because regulars don't know how to fight worth a damn,' Bill Anderson said.

The men agreed.

'That's the way I think too,' Quantrill said after a few moments. 'And I know that from personal experience. What happened at Pleasant Hill is proof that our men can fight four, maybe six times their numbers, and still come out ahead.'

Todd got up and, going to the hearth, let fly a mouthful of tobacco juice. Then standing close to the table, he said, 'We all know how ya beat da blue-bellies. Get on wid wot ya made us come all dis way for.' He walked slowly back to his seat on a straight-backed chair, not far from the door. 'I propose we take Lawrence,' he said.

The effect was instantaneous: all the men began to talk at the same time. Quantrill rapped his revolver on the table several times, but it did no good. He glanced at Thomas, who took a step forward and was about to shout for silence, when John Jarrette called out, 'Let's listen to what the colonel has to say.'

The noise lessened and then stopped. Quantrill told them that by taking Lawrence, they would force the Union to lessen the pressure on Lee. Troops would have to be withdrawn from the east.

'We got a bellyful of blue-bellies in these parts,' Dick Maddox said. The others agreed with him.

But Quantrill continued to talk. 'All the plunder or at least the bulk of it, stolen from Missouri will be found stored away in Lawrence,' he told his subordinates. 'We can get more revenge and more money there than anywhere else in Kansas.'

Thomas quickly realized that Quantrill had held his winning card for the last. The mention of loot was too much for the raiders to resist. It overrode whatever fears they might have had about such a foray.

Finally Quantrill said, 'I know the hazards this enterprise bears, but if you never risk, you never gain.'

There was too much of the gambler in each of the men for them to resist the challenge. And though there was arguing about details for several hours, everyone in the room agreed that they would attack Lawrence on August twenty-first.

The long column of almost five hundred men began its march from Lone Jack, Missouri to Lawrence, Kansas on the eighteenth of August. At its head rode Quantrill, and directly behind him came Thomas.

The other leaders rode in front of their own bands of men. And the Confederate Regulars, about a hundred strong, were led by Colonel Holt, who according to Quantrill had been sent by General Sterling Price to take part in the raid.

'Kind of gives it the official stamp of approval,' Quantrill laughed, when he told Thomas about it some days prior to the eighteenth.

Quantrill saw to it that every raider was well mounted and double armed, either with two revolvers or a combination of a revolver and a carbine. Some even carried all three. All of the raiders wore butternut-colored trousers and jackets and wide-brimmed slouch hats. They were lean and ferocious-looking men. Their respective leaders had told them about the loot that awaited them in Lawrence, and they were more than anxious to get their hands on it.

On the night of August twentieth, Quantrill halted the column. The light from a first-quarter moon threw the shadows of the lean men on their mounts over the dry Kansas earth.

Quantrill ordered all of the men, raiders and regulars alike, to form a huge semi-circle around him. When they were where he wanted them, he stood up in the stirrups and said, 'Tomorrow night at this time we will have taken Lawrence and retrieved that which has been stolen from us.'

The men growled their agreement.

'What I want you to do here and now,' Quantrill said removing his slouch hat, 'in the presence of your fellow men and in sight of God Almighty, is to swear that come tomorrow, when we ride into Lawrence, that each of you will do what is necessary to win a great victory for our cause. I want you to swear to show the Union in blood that there are still men who will stand and fight for their cherished beliefs, for their land and for their right to maintain slaves, if that is what they believe is best for them.'

There was passion in Quantrill's voice. He sounded like a great, deep-voiced bell. The way he spoke reminded Thomas of Mr Coomy, who also believed that the South's cause was righteous and had absolutely no doubt that God was on the side of the Confederacy.

'Raise your right hands,' Quantrill shouted out, his voice more intense than ever, 'and say after me: "I solemnly swear to fight for the Confederate cause and if God so wills, to die for it."'

Just as the moon set, the men swore. Moments later the march was resumed under a black sky studded with more stars than Thomas could count in a lifetime.

The men seldom spoke to each other. There was little need for words. All of them, to a man, knew what lay ahead. Other than the low sound of hooves and the squeak of leather moving against leather, the long column slithered snake-like across the open prairie.

Sometime around midnight, Quantrill ordered a halt. No fires were allowed and the men, wrapped in blankets to stave off the chill of the night air, lay down for a few hours' rest.

With the first light they were up again. Taking time to eat some hard tack and jerked beef, they were in their saddles again and on their way before the full yellow circle of the sun cleared the eastern horizon.

By eight o'clock in the morning several outriders ran into Union vedettes, and after a sharp exchange of gunfire that killed two of them and left one outrider badly wounded, the remaining Union troops galloped away.

News of the encounter infuriated Quantrill. He had given all of them a standing order to avoid making contact with the enemy, lest such an action betray the column. 'If it were not for the fact that we need every man,' he told the outrider, 'I'd kill you myself. Now get back to your units.'

A few minutes later he turned his attention to Thomas and said, 'I was hoping to surprise them. Now it seems as though they'll be ready and waiting for us.'

'I guess there's a chance of that happening,' Thomas answered, not knowing what else he could say.

Quantrill lowered his lids and looked very angry, but he just shook his head and faced front. But after a few minutes, he changed the direction of march. And he continued to do that several times during the rest of the morning, though for all the different movements, they continued to ride in a west-by-north direction.

The sun was hot, the air dry and the men were thirsty. But none of them dared complain or take water from his canteen.

Late in the morning, the column reached a farmhouse. Quantrill ordered one of his men to rout the farmer out and, at gunpoint, forced the man to guide the raiders through a twisting maze of creeks and gullies. The farmer mistakenly told Quantrill that he was a peaceful man, favoring neither the Union nor the Confederacy.

'A man has to believe in one or the other,' Quantrill said.

'The South then,' the man answered.

'You're a lying son-of-a-bitch!' Quantrill exclaimed and without saying anything else he drew and shot him.

During the day outriders brought several more guides to the column and sooner or later Quantrill had each of them shot, under the pretext that they were purposefully leading the raiders away from Lawrence or toward the Union troops.

Quantrill ordered the marching pace quickened. The men grumbled. They were tired and saddle sore. Then Todd came galloping up to Quantrill and said that his men would feel a lot better if they had time to rest.

'I don't want them to feel a lot better,' Quantrill told him. 'I want them to be madder than hell when they get to Lawrence. That way I'll know they'll do God's work when they get there.'

Todd pulled the brim of his slouched hat down over his squinting eyes, when suddenly two of the outriders came galloping toward the head of the column, and with them was a third rider — a man who they had seen, chased and captured.

The man identified himself as Joseph Smith. He seemed to know Quantrill, and was definitely afraid of him.

'Can't let him go,' Todd said, looking at the helpless man.

'We're too close to Lawrence to shoot him,' Quantrill commented.

Todd swung off his horse and, going over to Joseph Smith, pulled the man from the saddle, letting him fall to the ground. Then he calmly unslung his Sharps rifle and, before Smith could cry out, drove the butt into the man's head. The first blow stunned him and broke the skin on the scalp, staining the butt red. The second and third blows actually smashed the man's skull. By the fifth blow, Smith was dead and his bloody brains were splattered on the brown earth. Then Todd knelt down and wiped the bloodstains off the Sharps on the dead man's jacket.

As soon as Todd remounted he looked straight at Quantrill and said, 'That's just about how angry my men are.' Then he wheeled his horse around and galloped back to his unit.

By five o'clock the column crossed the border into Kansas. Quantrill pointed to a group of buildings over which flew the Union flag. 'That's Captain Pike's detachment,' he explained to Thomas. 'He'll stay put until we're past, and then probably send word to Kansas City that he's spotted us. But by that time we'll be finished with our work.'

When the column passed through Gardner, Kansas, which stood astride the Santa Fe Trail, it was eleven o'clock. The raiders paused long enough to burn several houses. The men who tried to fight back were killed.

The raiders reached Hesper by three o'clock in the morning. And because the night was pitch black, Quantrill took a young man at gunpoint to guide the column the rest of the way to Lawrence.

After a short ride, Quantrill and Thomas breasted the hill that overlooked the city. He signaled the column to halt and then told Thomas to take another man from the first group and go into Lawrence to reconnoiter.

Fifteen minutes later Thomas and the other raider were walking their mounts slowly up the main street. Except for the saloons, which were open all night, everything else was closed and dark. Nothing indicated that the citizens of Lawrence had the slightest suspicion about what would shortly happen to them.

When Thomas and the other man reached the end of the street, they swung around the courthouse and started back.

'It's goin' to be easy,' the other raider said with a low laugh.

'It looks that way,' Thomas answered.

'I hear tell ya wuz with the colonel at Pleasant Hill,' the rider said.

Thomas nodded and the obvious admiration in the young long-faced man brought a grudging smile to his lips.

The man reached across to Thomas and, offering his hand, said, 'I'm proud to know you, lootenant. Mah name is Frank James.'

'Thomas Carey.'

The two men shook hands, then, spurring their mounts, galloped out of Lawrence to tell Quantrill what he was waiting to hear.

ELEVEN

According to plan, Colonel Holt and his regulars left the column, first to strike at the small detachment of troops on the Lawrence side of the Kansas river, and then to hold that flank against a possible attack from a much larger force of soldiers, who were quartered just across the river. As soon as Holt and his men were in position, he would fire a single shot and that would be the signal for Quantrill to begin his assault on the city itself.

From what Thomas could see, a good many of the raiders looked as though they were asleep in their saddles. But there was a tenseness in the air that belied the apparent exhaustion of the men. Even the horses were restless, sensing that something was about to happen.

Quantrill turned to Thomas. 'Pass the word,' he said, 'that we begin at a trot as soon as the signal shot is fired.'

Thomas swung around and delivered the message to the men of the first group. Then he rode back to where Quantrill was.

'In a little while,' Quantrill said, moving his hand in front of him to encompass the city below the rise on which they were poised, 'all of that will be in flames.' He looked at Thomas. 'And we will have given the Confederacy a victory!'

Thomas nodded, but he suddenly wished that he was somewhere else. The whole idea of putting Lawrence to the torch made no sense to him. What Quantrill would consider a victory for the Confederacy would, he was certain, not only call down the wrath of the Union forces on them, but also that of the Confederate government.

He was annoyed with himself for not even attempting to dissuade Quantrill from going ahead with his plans to burn and loot the city. And if he could not have stopped him, Thomas felt that at least he should not have helped him or have agreed to take part in the raid.

Just as Thomas shook his head a single, sharp report snapped through the darkness of the night.

Instantly Quantrill spurred his mount to a trot. Thomas followed, and behind came the sound of many hooves beating on the slope of the hill as they rode down toward the city of Lawrence.

'Get your arms ready!' Quantrill shouted, pressing his horse to a gallop.

Thomas drew his revolver and spurred his mount.

The sound of the galloping raiders sounded like a low roll of thunder. Even as they rushed into the town and swept down Rhode Island Street, there were quick bursts of carbine fire from the river side.

Dividing into small groups of five or six men, the raiders spun off in every direction. The sound of gunfire was everywhere. The killing had already begun, and those townsmen who rushed out into the street were instantly cut down.

Quantrill swung up Massachusetts Street. Thomas was hard after him. Other raiders followed them, firing at anything and everything that moved. Men and women were running for safety. Along the river's edge, and at the other end of the city, buildings were burning.

Directly in front of the Eldridge House, Quantrill reined his mount and swung down from the saddle. He paused and waited for Thomas to join him. Then he gestured toward the silent building and asked, 'You think it's a trap?'

But before Thomas could answer, a man called out from a second-floor window. He identified himself as Captain A R Banks, Provost Marshall of Kansas. 'And,' he cried, 'I am willing to surrender.' A few moments later a white sheet was pushed through an open window.

'All right,' Quantrill shouted. 'I accept your surrender. Everyone inside will march out with their hands behind their heads. If one of you attempts to run or shoot, all of you will be killed.'

A few minutes later the occupants of the Eldridge House came out, and Quantrill told Thomas and several other men to take them over to the City Hotel, which was just across the street. Then he ordered the Eldridge House burned.

As soon as Thomas made sure that the people in his charge were safe inside the City Hotel, he took to the street again. By this time Quantrill had ordered all the male occupants of the Johnson House shot. More and more of Lawrence was put to the torch.

Some of the raiders had managed to get their hands on whiskey, and were killing in a blind drunken stupor. Wherever they found male citizens, no matter what their age, the raiders shot them.

Thomas did not re-join Quantrill; instead he started to move toward the river, where Colonel Holt and his regulars were still guarding against a flank attack.

The blackness of the night gave way to a reddish-yellow glow that seemed to come from the very heart of the city. Thomas slipped down a side street, then suddenly heard a woman scream. He stopped and turned toward a small wooden house. Through the window he saw two of the raiders had grabbed a woman. He ran toward the door, kicked it in. One of the raiders wheeled around.

Thomas fired. The bullet struck the man in the heart, killing him instantly. The other man still held the woman.

'Let go of her!' Thomas ordered.

'You ain't goin' to get away with this,' the man said.

'Let go of her!'

The raider released the woman and ran for the door. 'I'll see you in hell,' he shouted, and spinning around, he fired.

Thomas rushed at the woman and knocked her down, though not before a bullet grazed his right cheek. He returned the fire but the raider was gone. Wiping his bloody cheek with his sleeve, Thomas realized there was another man on the floor. He bent over him.

'Is he dead?' the woman asked with a sob.

'Yes,' Thomas said.

Mindless of her torn dress, she ran to the body and threw herself across it. 'He tried to stop them,' she cried looking up at Thomas, 'but they killed him … they killed Jim … they killed my husband.' Cradling the man's body, she held him close to her bare breasts and wept. But even as she cried, a small girl came out from behind the door of another room and also started to weep.

'See to the child,' Thomas told the woman, pulling her away from the body. 'Keep the house dark, and if anyone comes to the door, shoot.' And he handed her the revolver of the dead raider.

Moments later he was in the street again, but by this time he had changed his mind, and instead of going to Colonel Holt he went to find Quantrill. The raiders had done their worst to Lawrence, and if anything was to be saved Quantrill would have to call them off. Even if it meant a showdown with him, Thomas was determined to put a stop to the raid.

He found Quantrill was waiting for him. 'Don't try anything,' he warned Thomas, 'or you'll be a dead man.'

Thomas stopped and raised his hands.

'You're a fool, lieutenant,' Quantrill said, looking through the narrow slit of his lowered lids, 'if you shot one of my men.'

'I should have killed the both of them,' Thomas said, 'they were going to rape —'

'That was their right!' Quantrill said sharply.

'Not the way I see it,' Thomas answered, shaking his head. 'What's happened here is bad enough —'

'If it were anyone else,' Quantrill said, 'I would have him shot or hung. But I owe you my life. I will pay that debt here and now. Mount up and ride, lieutenant … and if I ever see you again, one of us will die.'

Thomas nodded, turned and walked slowly down the flame-lit street to his horse. Moments later he was in the saddle and galloping out of the burning city of Lawrence. He never once looked back.

This time he was heading straight toward the Cherokee strip, and Texas.

TWELVE

By the early autumn, Thomas reached the Arkansas River and headed for Little Rock, a day's ride downstream. By waiting for a night when it rained so hard and was so black that only a desperate man would risk riding through unfamiliar country, he had managed to slip through the Union patrols on the Missouri border some weeks earlier.

Though Thomas had discarded the butternut-colored trousers and jacket that had marked him as one of Quantrill's raiders, the bullet that had grazed his cheek that night in Lawrence had left a scar that even his beard could not hide. But on the afternoon he rode into Little Rock, he still wore a slouched hat and carried his gun low on his right thigh. He knew that he looked lean and dangerous, but so did hundreds of other men on the streets of Little Rock. And he had no doubt that many were deserters from both of the contending armies.

Compared to most of the places Thomas had seen in the last few years, Little Rock was a busy city that for a price offered a man anything he could want. The main street was lined with saloons, gambling houses and dance halls. More often than not all three conveniences were under one roof.

After delivering his horse to a livery stable for care, Thomas took a room in a modest hotel on Main Street. Then he purchased a whole set of new clothes, returned to his room, and took a long hot bath. Dressed in his new togs, he went out to look around.

There was a kind of madness in the city. Everyone seemed hell-bent on having a good time, making the most of what there was. Maybe it was because the war was going bad for the South and the people were living through a bad dream.

When night came, the city glowed from countless lamps and burning torches. There were crowds milling around in pursuit of pleasure. But there were also those gaunt men in Confederate gray whose presence was a grim reminder of the war, and all the horror it had meant and would continue to mean to all of them, until the last shot was fired and the last man killed.

But Thomas saw that a great deal of money — not Confederate scrip but Yankee gold — passed hands. Those men who supplied the army demanded and were paid in hard money. And those men who stayed at the gaming tables took their winnings or paid their losses in gold and silver dollars.

After the weeks of traveling alone, Thomas found himself enjoying the excitement that was all around him, and he decided rather than leave in a day or two as he had originally planned, he would stay on in Little Rock and enjoy himself, which was something he had not done in a long time.

He walked the streets until midnight and then, on the way back to his hotel, he stopped for a drink in a saloon called the Creole Beauty. The bar room was enormous. A crystal chandelier with more candles on it than he had ever seen hung suspended from the ceiling by four heavy-linked chains. And there were coal-oil lamps all over the room. Off to the right was a staircase that led to the upper floors, where the patrons of the establishment could find relaxation and pleasure with one of the house women. Off to the left was a gaming room, where a man could sit in on a poker game, or play faro or roulette.

But the bar itself was most commanding. It occupied the entire back wall. It was darkly stained and so highly polished that it caught the shimmering light from the chandelier. Behind it, the wall was divided into three parts. The center portion held a large painting of a naked woman in a reclining position.

There was little of her body that the artist hadn't managed to reveal, everything from the erect nipples on her full breasts, to the dark, kinky hair above her womanhood. He also had cleverly made sure that anyone who ever looked at the painting would immediately know that the woman in it was not white, but rather some dark-skinned beauty. And on either side of the painting there was a mirror, angled out from the wall just enough to reflect the painting, giving the overall effect of three identical paintings.

Thomas went up to the bar and stared at the painting for some time before he ordered a whiskey. Other than some brief contacts with prostitutes in Kansas City, he had not had any sort of relationship with a woman. But the painting started him thinking about Jenny, as her skin was about the same color as that of the woman in the painting. And she was put together the same way, with full breasts, good hips and shapely legs.

He ordered another drink and rested his foot on the brass rail at the bottom of the bar. If there was ever anyone to whom he owed his life, he knew it was Jenny. And though he had left her, he would never forget her.

His thoughts were just about to turn to Lisa, who at that moment he longed to see with such intensity that he would have changed his mind about staying more than the night in Little Rock, if he hadn't become aware of the fact that a man not ten feet away was staring at him. Slowly he removed his foot from the railing and, turning to his right, faced the stranger.

The man nodded and smiled. He was a tall, broad-shouldered, heavy-set fellow, with black hair and bushy eyebrows. He wore a side arm. 'I didn't mean to stare at you,' he said. 'But you look familiar.'

Thomas acknowledged the apology with a nod. 'I'm afraid you have the advantage,' he said. 'I just arrived in town this afternoon.'

'Well now,' the man said, 'if'n that ain't somethin'! I came in today myself. I'm just out of the army. Took a Yankee bullet in my side.' The man introduced himself as Charles Nesbit and offered to buy Thomas a drink.

'Only if you let me repay the kindness,' Thomas said.

Mr Nesbit nodded and moved closer to Thomas. 'It's mighty hard to tell,' he commented, 'from the way things are in this city, that there's a war going on.'

Thomas agreed.

After the barkeep brought their drinks, Nesbit drank to the success of the Southern cause. Then he said, 'I can't help feelin' that I've seen you before.'

Thomas shook his head.

'There wuz this man,' Nesbit commented, 'a Yankee —'

'I'm from Paso Diablo, Texas,' Thomas told him. 'I don't have any kin in the north.'

Nesbit pulled his ear. 'I'm real good at rememberin' faces,' he said. 'And I've seen yours, or somebody's that is your spittin' image.'

Thomas was becoming annoyed, but he tried not to show it. He bought the second round of drinks and when they finished drinking, he told Nesbit that he would be staying in Little Rock for a few days before riding home. Then he thanked him for the drink and said goodnight.

He was several steps from the bar when Nesbit called out, 'Say, mister, you didn't give me your name.'

Thomas turned, and would have told him that it was none of his business, but then Nesbit snapped his fingers.

'It's come back to me!' he exclaimed. 'It wasn't you I seen, but a Yankee captain. John Carey,' Nesbit exclaimed with great satisfaction, 'that was the bastard's name!'

Hearing his brother's name mentioned made Thomas feel weak in the knees. To rid himself of the tightness in his throat, he coughed several times, and then he moved slowly back to the bar.

'I told you,' Nesbit said, 'I got a way of rememberin' names and faces.'

'What about John Carey?' Thomas asked in a low voice.

Nesbit shrugged.

Thomas repeated the question.

'Nothing about him,' Nesbit said, looking questioningly at Thomas. 'Besides, what difference does it make to you. He wuz a damn Yankee and you —'

Thomas grabbed hold of the man's arm. 'What about John Carey?' he said again. But this time his voice roared out.

Nesbit pulled away. 'You got no call to act that way, mister,' he complained. 'I come over to you nice and friendly.'

'I want to know about John Carey,' Thomas said.

'Don't push me,' Nesbit answered. 'I ain't about to be pushed by the likes of you.'

Thomas didn't answer.

'This whole damn thing ain't worth arguing about,' he said. 'What the hell difference does it make about one more dead Yankee captain?' And he looked around the room at the other men to confirm what he had said.

'Dead?' Thomas whispered. And then he yelled, 'John dead?'

Nesbit's eyes opened wide and his jaw went slack.

'How,' Thomas asked, 'how did it happen?'

Nesbit shook his head.

'I want to know,' Thomas said.

Nesbit shook his head again.

'Leave him alone,' one of the men on the sidelines called out.

'This is none of your affair,' Thomas answered without looking at the man. 'This is between Mister Nesbit and myself.'

'I don't even know you,' Nesbit said. 'I don't even know this man. I was just bein' friendly —'

'I'm John's brother, Thomas.'

Nesbit's hand dropped toward his holster. But Thomas' gun was already out, and the repercussion of the single shot made the glasses on the bar jump.

Nesbit dropped to his knees, looking up at Thomas, and with blood gurgling out of his mouth managed to say, 'He was an enemy … he tried to run … I did what I had to do … I did…'

'He was my brother!' Thomas shouted. 'He was my brother!'

And he continued to pull the trigger until someone shouted, 'For God's sakes, how many times do you want to kill him?'

'Once is hardly enough,' he answered, holding the smoking revolver in front of him. 'By the living God, once is hardly enough!' And as he walked slowly out of the saloon, and the men moved aside to let him pass, he heard some of them claim that it was a fair fight, while others said he should be lynched for killing a man who had only done his duty.

Thomas left Little Rock long before the dawn came. He rode south toward home.

THIRTEEN

The knowledge that John was dead made Thomas ache with grief. And as he rode south by west toward the Texas border, he felt as though he were being forced to shoulder an insupportable burden. The yellow days with their bright blue skies were fused together by the links of the star-studded nights, during which he halted for a few hours' sleep. But his dreams robbed him of his sleep.

Sometimes he would see John as he had when he went to Richmond to visit him in Libby Prison and John had said, 'If I don't make it, promise me that your next son will have my name.'

'I will, John,' Thomas had answered with a nod.

'A man likes to know that he leaves something behind,' John had said with a smile before the guard hustled him out of the small, bare visiting room.

Sometimes in his dreams John would stand in front of him, then hunker down and tell him how their grandfather sired a bastard, and how their father was afraid that his own sons might have tainted blood.

'The old man was afraid of that,' John said. 'And that fear made him into a hard, unloving and ungiving man. But you Thomas, you have something of our father in you.'

'No.'

John nodded and said, 'You both love the land.'

'It's not enough.'

'Maybe if you give it time ... you were always his favorite, always the one he knew would stay with him...'

But Thomas told his brother about Zeb. 'Pa sent Zeb to kill me,' Thomas cried. 'And I'm going back to kill him.'

And then he thought of Lisa, and the night she had learned that Helen was pregnant. That same night, Lisa had demanded that he leave Helen and live with her permanently.

'No,' he had answered. 'I told you no more times than I can count.'

'It is because of the child?'

'No,' Thomas shouted. 'I want what's mine. Do you understand that?' He smashed his fist down on the table. 'My blood and my sweat are in that land. I was just a kid when I started to work ... my father made me ride before I learned to read or write.'

'You want too much,' Lisa shouted back. 'You want me, your wife, your child, the ranch — what else do you want?'

'Just to be left alone,' he roared back at her. 'Just to be left alone, you whoring bitch!'

The dreams left him wide awake and wet with perspiration. And more often than not, he'd saddle up and begin to ride, using the stars to guide him through the darkness.

Two weeks after he left Little Rock he rode into the town of Texarkana, where he stopped for a day to rest himself and his horse.

There he learned that Quantrill and his men had attempted to raid Sherman, a small town in northern Texas, but were beaten off with heavy losses. There were many stories bruited about how Quantrill was taken prisoner by General Henry McCulloch and then made a miraculous escape, only to be shot down in a running gun battle.

Thomas could easily believe the first part of the story, but it hardly seemed likely that Quantrill would have been foolish enough to risk his life over such lean pickings as Sherman.

The next morning, when the yellow rim of the sun began to show in the east, Thomas was on his way again. A few days later he forded the Sabine River. He was becoming more and more anxious to reach his goal. And the closer he came to it, the stronger he was beginning to feel.

The terrible grief he had experienced after learning about John's death eased considerably, and even the bad dreams left him. Maybe it was because he was so set in his mind about doing what had to be done. Whatever the reason, Thomas was feeling better than he had in a long time.

When he left the Brazos River behind him, Thomas found himself in the kind of country he had known most of his life. For the most part it was flat, open and dry. He saw a great many strays in the bush, and now and again he passed a burned-out ranch house. But as he came closer to the Llano River, the strays became more numerous, and so did the burned and deserted ranches. Then late one morning, when the sky was filled with gray clouds and there was a bite in the air that was a clear sign that summer was over, Thomas spotted a plume of black smoke several miles to the west.

His first thought was that the smoke was coming from a brush fire. But it was a good two months past the season for lightning storms that were usually the cause of such fires. The more he looked at the smoke, the more unlike brush fire smoke it seemed. His curiosity aroused, Thomas turned his horse and rode toward it at a trot.

The land sloped toward the river and rose again on the other side. As Thomas breasted the hill, he looked down and saw a burning ranch house. He unslung his carbine and spurred his mount to a gallop.

A few minutes later, he was out of the saddle and walking across the front yard. There was a dead man in the doorway, with an arrow in his chest and his scalp missing. Thomas stepped over him.

A boy of fifteen or sixteen lay dead in a pool of blood near the rough wooden table. His scalp had been taken too.

Directly in front of the hearth was a woman. What had been done to her before she had been killed and scalped was all too obvious from the way her clothes were torn.

The back of the house was still burning, and the fire was beginning to spread into the front room along the wooden roofbeams. From the arrow, Thomas knew that it was the work of a Comanche war party. Ever since he had entered Texas and had met up with men in the towns or drifters along the way, he had heard stories about how Union agents had stirred up the Indians throughout all of Texas, giving them guns and whiskey, which was the worst possible combination.

Thomas hadn't paid too much heed to the stories, but as he went about the grim task of burying the members of the family, he knew that what he had heard was all too true.

After he marked each grave with a crude cross, he stood looking down at them for several moments. Thomas' utter disbelief in the Almighty prevented him from experiencing anything remotely resembling a religious thought, and he had seen too much of death to feel any emotion over the demise of the three people he had just buried. As he stood there, he realized that if the Indians had been stirred up by Union agents, they had foolishly sown the seeds for future violence between the Indians and the settlers in the southwest. What may have seemed the right thing to do during the war would reap a bloody harvest of death for both the Indian and the white man in the years to come.

Thomas shook his head and, picking up his carbine, he glanced at the crest of the hill where he had paused just a short while ago to look down at the burning house. He saw a half-dozen braves galloping down the slope.

Thomas ran for his horse, mounted up and galloped off. There was little or no chance of his mount outrunning the swift Indian ponies, and unless he managed to get to some decent cover, he couldn't make any sort of stand.

The only real cover was behind him, along the river. But in order to reach it, he would either have to make a wide circle which would give the Indians the advantage, or he could turn around and meet them head on. They wouldn't expect that, and if he was lucky he might be able to kill enough of them to give better odds for an escape when he reached the river.

Thomas glanced over his shoulder. The braves were hot on his tail. They were shouting and gesturing wildly at him.

He leaned low over his saddle and spurred his mount so violently that it did manage to gallop faster.

The high-pitched whine of an arrow rose above the pounding beat of horse hooves. The slender shaft flew past him and then dropped away. Another followed. This one kept pace with him for a few moments, then it too dropped.

He sensed that his pursuers were gaining, and expected to feel the stab of a flint arrowhead in his back at any moment. If he was going to turn, he would have to do it within the next few moments. He laid his carbine across the pommel and hoped to be able to bring it up to his shoulder as soon as he maneuvered his mount around.

But just as he pulled the reins to the left and the horse began to veer around, he saw that the war party had dropped back and was riding hard off to the right. And the next instant he saw a dozen riders moving in on them from the left.

He reined in his lathered mount and, patting its trembling flanks, watched the chase.

Suddenly the sound of rifle fire broke the silence of the plain. Three of the six braves dropped from their ponies. Another fusillade brought down two more. A single shot got the remaining Indian.

The riders slowed and turned toward Thomas, while he slowly moved toward them. He owed them the courtesy of a 'thank you'. If they hadn't arrived on the scene, Thomas doubted that he would have succeeded in escaping.

The leader of the band, a chunky, barrel-chested man with a brown, drooping mustache and brown eyes, introduced himself as Bud McTavish. He told Thomas that he and the rest of the men were ranchers in the area and when they saw the smoke from the Hubbards' place they knew what had happened. 'Then we jest figured,' he explained, 'that we'd get together and go after the red devils. We saw you first, and then the Indians.'

'I'm sure glad you came along,' Thomas said.

Mr McTavish confirmed what Thomas had already heard about the Indian trouble. 'And it's not likely to end when the war does. No, sir, it's goin' to be a war all its own.'

Thomas agreed.

'I don't mean to be pokin' around in your business,' McTavish said, 'but ridin' alone isn't exactly safe, especially if you don't know the country.'

'I'm going home,' Thomas said.

McTavish cocked his head to one side.

'I have a ranch just outside of Paso Diablo,' Thomas explained. 'Maybe you heard of the WC brand?'

'Sure have!' McTavish exclaimed. Then suddenly he slapped his thigh and said, 'I should have guessed you were comin' home from the war. Should have known it. By God, even if you aren't wearin' a uniform, we don't have too many young men around these parts anymore. Most of them are gone to fight. Then you must be one of the Carey boys?'

'Thomas Carey,' he answered.

McTavish shook his hand and announced who the stranger was to the other men. Then he said, 'I know you're anxious to be on your way, but from the shape of your mount and yourself, you could use some rest. My wife Sarah and I would be right proud if you spent the night at our place.'

Thomas shook his head.

'Our boy went off to fight,' McTavish said. 'Run away when he jest turned sixteen.' The man shook his head. 'Sarah would be angry with me if she knew that I didn't invite you…'

Thomas suddenly remembered the young boy without shoes on the march to the railhead. And though he knew that the boy couldn't have been McTavish's son, he found himself saying that he would indeed like to spend the night at the man's home. 'But only if you're sure,' Thomas added, 'that I won't cause any upset.'

'It will make Sarah happy,' McTavish said.

Thomas nodded, and as he went along with McTavish and the rest of the men, he had the peculiar feeling that he was paying a debt he owed to that young soldier without shoes.

The McTavish spread was not very large, but the ranch house was well built and much like Thomas' own home. There was a good-sized dining room almost immediately beyond the front door. A smaller sitting room was off to the left and the kitchen to the right. The doors to the bedrooms flanked the huge hearth. The rooms were well furnished and kept neat and clean.

Mrs McTavish was a small, plumpish woman who was delighted to have Thomas as a guest and proved it by the dinner she put on the table that night. There was more food than Thomas had seen in several years. Mr McTavish took out a jug of good corn whiskey.

For the first time since he had left Jenny, Thomas sat down to eat without wearing his gun. And several times throughout the meal his right hand dropped down to his thigh to feel for the very thing he had removed. He was certain that Mr McTavish caught sight of his furtive searchings.

Mr McTavish bowed his head and said grace before dinner, and though Thomas lowered his eyes respectfully, he felt easier when the short prayer was over.

After Mrs McTavish served the soup, she sat down and, looking at Thomas, asked him about the war.

'Don't do that, Mother,' her husband said. 'The man is going home … he don't want to think about the past.'

Thomas nodded respectfully toward Mr McTavish and then he said to the woman, 'I don't really know what to tell you. I was a lieutenant in the cavalry … we rode hard, and I guess we fought hard.'

'By golly,' Mr McTavish exclaimed, 'I figured you were in the cavalry just from the way you ride!'

'That's more from being a Texan,' Thomas answered, 'than from anything I learned in the army.'

'My son ran off —'

'Now, Mother,' Mr McTavish said, 'Thomas didn't meet up with our Billy. Soon he'll be comin' home.'

Mrs McTavish nodded and apologized for bringing up her personal problems. Thomas nodded understandingly, but he could tell from the look in the woman's eyes that somewhere deep inside of herself she wept, and probably would continue to weep for the rest of her life.

Thomas told them about Richmond and Little Rock. Toward the end of the dinner Mrs McTavish asked Thomas if the scar on his face came from a Yankee bullet. He lied and said it did.

Then, after the table was cleared and Mr McTavish offered Thomas a cigar, the talk swung away from Thomas' particular role in the war to the broader picture of the conflict. Though Mr McTavish was for the Confederacy, he was level-headed enough to realize that the South would be better off surrendering than fighting until she was beaten to her knees. But then he added, 'Not too many people hold to that. They reckon that we still can win.'

Thomas shook his head and, in a quiet voice, said, 'I don't think we can. The Union can put more guns in the field than we can.'

'Then why in the name of the dear Lord,' Mrs McTavish exclaimed, 'are we fighting a war we can't win?'

Thomas shrugged and said, 'I don't really know.'

'But,' the woman said, coming up to the table, 'why did you go?'

Thomas heaved a deep sigh and looked down at the polished wood of the table. 'Now that I think of it,' he said, 'I was just plain stupid.' He raised his eyes and looked at Mrs McTavish. 'At. the time it seemed as though it was the only thing I could do, if you know what I mean?'

'Every man who called himself a man,' Mr McTavish said, 'had to go.'

'No,' Thomas commented, shaking his head. 'No, that wasn't it at all … at least not where I was concerned.'

The two people looked at him questioningly.

'It gave me a chance to get away,' he said, 'and that's what I wanted to do. War does that, you know … it makes all sorts of things possible, and most of them are senseless. Maybe all of them are.'

When the conversation lapsed into long silences, Mr McTavish suggested that they turn in and he showed Thomas to the room that had been his son's. They said goodnight and shook hands.

Thomas fell into a deep sleep, but around midnight he awoke with a start. He had been dreaming again, but as soon as he was awake the dream passed out of his memory. Toward morning he drifted off to sleep again.

The good scent of frying bacon and hot coffee woke him, and after breakfasting with the McTavishes he thanked them for their hospitality and took his leave, though not before Mr McTavish insisted that he take a cow pony. 'Yours is all tuckered out, and besides, you might run into another band of Indians and need some good horse flesh under your saddle.'

Thomas knew that it would be useless to argue, and he accepted Mr McTavish's offer, but only after he made it quite clear that not only would the animal be returned but with it would come some other gift. Finally Thomas was mounted and ready to go. He waved goodbye to Mrs McTavish, who was standing in the open doorway, and then reached down to shake his host's hand.

'You know,' the man said looking up at Thomas, 'I spent a lot of time last night thinkin' about you.'

'Oh?'

'I was thinkin',' Mr McTavish said, 'that with all your talkin' last night you never made mention of your kinfolk — or, for that matter, about the ranch.'

Thomas eased his hand out of the other man's hold.

'I figure,' McTavish told him, 'that if a man takes so much trouble to ride all the way home, he must love his place and his people very much. But you don't have that look.'

'What kind of look do I have?' Thomas asked.

'Like a man hell-bent to do something. It's kind of burned into your face jest like that scar. And for your sake,' he said, 'I hope it's for God and not against Him.'

Mr McTavish's words took Thomas by surprise, but rather than answer, he nodded, whispered a parting 'Thank you.' Then, wheeling his horse around, he trotted out of the front yard.

FOURTEEN

Three days after Thomas left the McTavish ranch he crossed the Nueces River and swung west toward Paso Diablo. Though he desperately wanted to see Lisa, he bypassed the town and rode instead to the ranch, where he had business to settle with his father.

The day was bright, with sun and cotton-like puffs of clouds sailing across a bright blue sky. A wind was blowing and balls of tumbleweed rolled over the flat open country.

Thomas stayed off the main road that lay between Paso Diablo and the ranch. Much of the vegetation was already brown, another sign that winter would soon be hard on the land. And he caught sight of many strays in the bushes along the way.

The closer he came to the ranch, the straighter he sat in the saddle and the firmer became the set of his jaw. He felt empty, but at the same time there was the same tenseness in his gut that he had always experienced before a battle.

By the time he caught sight of the ranch, the sun was high in the sky. He stood on the ridge just beyond the long slope that ended at the rough wooden fence. His first impulse was to gallop into the front yard and storm into the house … call his father out, tell the old man about Zeb and then kill him.

But then he had another thought.

He would ride down the slope at a walk. Maybe Helen, his wife, or the old man would see him. He'd enter the front yard, secure his mount to the hitching post and enter the house with the same kind of nonchalance that he might have had if he had

just returned from a trip to town. Nothing loud or violent —
at least not until he threw down on the old man and pulled the
trigger.

Thomas nodded and decided to wait until sundown before
going down to the house. He moved back behind the ridge and
rode off to the south. And then he saw Helen. She was
standing under a large tree that had already lost most of its
foliage. He instantly knew it was her by the way her head lolled
off to the right side.

He sighed deeply. That was part of what Zeb had done to
her when he and his friends came to the ranch the night
Thomas and Helen had married. But he had paid Zeb back …
he had paid him back in spades.

Suddenly Thomas realized that Helen was standing where his
mother had been buried. He reined in. Why was she at his
mother's grave? She never knew the woman — and, for that
matter, neither did he. His mother had died shortly after giving
birth to him, and until he had reached the age when his father
had taken charge of him it had been Maria Gonzalez, the cook,
who had been his mother.

His mount snorted and moved nervously sideways. Thomas
steadied the animal, but made no attempt to go closer. He
watched her kneel and set the last of the summer's flowers on
the grave.

Even from a distance, Thomas could see that there was more
than one gravestone.

His heart began to race. His hands became wet with sweat.
He touched his spurs to the flanks of his mount and the animal
moved slowly toward the kneeling figure.

Eventually she stood up and turned. Gathering her black
cloak more securely around her, she waited for the rider to
come closer.

When he was still some distance from her, Thomas reined in. From where he was he saw that the other gravestone was a small one, the kind set to mark the grave of a child.

He nodded, as though agreeing with an inner voice that told him that his son was dead. Even as he acknowledged this, he felt no sharp pang of emotion. The boy had been an infant when he had left. What could he feel for a child he had never known, born from a woman whom he had not loved?

As these thoughts passed through his brain, Thomas realized that Helen was staring up at him. From the expression on her face, he knew that she was prodding her memory for some hint of his identity. He said nothing. The years hadn't changed her much. Her hair was still yellow, and she still wore it long to hide the place where Zeb had cut and branded her. The more he studied her, the more he realized that she had become more womanly in some respects. But there was something in her face and blue eyes that he had not remembered. It wasn't exactly a hardness, though some might take it for that. No, it was the look of a woman with a deep strength, the kind of flintiness that would have been more suitable to a much older woman.

'What do you want?' she suddenly challenged.

That she had not recognized him brought a thin smile to Thomas' lips, and he said, 'I would have thought you would have remembered.'

Her eyes opened wide and she gasped.

'Now you know,' he said swinging down from the saddle. He dropped the rein and walked toward her.

Thomas! she exclaimed. *Thomas.*

He stopped. 'I bet,' he said with a forced laugh, 'that neither you nor my pa ever expected to see me again.'

Helen came toward him. As soon as she moved, Thomas saw that there were three gravestones. Helen had been standing in front of the one that was next to his mother's.

She saw him staring at the graves. 'Ethan died in the spring,' she said in a low voice. 'Came down with a high fever and was gone in a couple of days.'

Thomas could see his father's name chiseled into the gray rock. He pointed to it and said, 'When did he die?'

'Not too long after the boy,' she told him.

Thomas walked past her and stood above the grave of his father. He shook his head … He should have known the old man wouldn't wait for him to come home. He clenched and unclenched his fists in suppressed fury. Almost a year he had been traveling — *traveling?* No, *scratching* his way home — so that he could kill him. Waiting for that exquisite moment when he would have faced the old bastard down and pulled the trigger. It had kept him alive … given him a purpose … made him ride several thousands of miles. And now it was not to be. The son-of-a-bitch couldn't even give him that much.

The cords on Thomas' neck gathered into hard vertical ridges. His breathing was hard and there was a huge knot in his throat.

'With his last breath, he called for you,' Helen told him.

Thomas glared at her for a moment and then looked back at his father's grave.

Shaking her head, Helen gently commented, 'It would not be unmanly for a son to weep for a father.'

He faced her. In a flat voice and with his eyes narrowed down to slits, he said, 'I came home to kill the son-of-a-bitch. I'm only sorry that he didn't live long enough to let me do it.'

Then he turned and walked back to his horse.

Helen ran after him. 'And you have nothing to say about your dead son?' she shouted.

'He was *your* son,' Thomas answered, swinging into the saddle again.

She grabbed hold of the bridle. 'He was from your loins, Thomas Carey,' she told him. 'Your seed.'

'I never knew him.'

'You never loved him.'

Thomas tried to turn his mount, but she held the bridle and the animal whinnied in confusion. He stopped and, looking down at her, said, 'I came home to kill the old man. Now there's no reason to stay.'

Helen let go of the bridle and, looking straight up at him, said, 'She's married. Lisa's married to the blacksmith. There's no sense going to town to see her.'

Thomas glared at her. But she didn't seem to be afraid of him. On the contrary, there was an unmistakable look of satisfaction on Helen's face. He shook his head and dismounted. Suddenly he was very tired and almost past caring about anything.

'Aren't you going to ask any questions?' she said.

He shook his head.

'We got word that you were missing in action,' she told him after a few moments of silence.

Thomas didn't answer. He handed the reins to her and walked back to the graves, where he stood for a long, long time without moving. And then, clenching his teeth so that the words would not be heard by anyone but himself, he said, 'Maybe John was right, Pa … maybe all we needed was time.'

Thomas wished he could have told his father that. The old man might have understood…

Then, heaving a deep sigh, Thomas turned. Taking the reins from Helen's hand, he walked slowly down to the house, with her at his side.

A NOTE TO THE READER

Dear Reader,
If you have enjoyed the novel enough to leave a review on **Amazon** and **Goodreads**, then we would be truly grateful.
Sapere Books

Sapere Books is an exciting new publisher of brilliant fiction and popular history.

To find out more about our latest releases and our monthly bargain books visit our website: **saperebooks.com**